PROBLEMS IN ANNADY'S CORE

PROBLEMS IN ANNADY'S CORE

Book 3 in the Dragons in Space Series

by Sandy Lender

*If you can convince people in their hearts
to look on the elements of our galaxy with compassion,
they'll be more likely to accept all with kindness.*

IYF Publishing/Dragon Hoard Press

IYF Publishing/Dragon Hoard Press
Florida
USA

This is a work of fiction. Names, characters, places, and incidents are products of the author's imagination or are used fictitiously and are not to be construed as real. Any resemblance to actual events, locales, organizations, or persons, living or dead, is entirely coincidental.

First edition published in USA, 2020.
Print ISBN 978-1-7345152-3-7
eBook ISBN 978-1-7345152-4-4
Cover design by Sandy Lender
Editor: Stephen Zimmer Author & Publishing Services

Other Works by Sandy Lender

Choices Meant for Gods
Choices Meant for Kings
Choices Meant for All
What Choices We Made, Vol I
What Choices We Made, Vol II

Problems on Eldora Prime
Problems above Pangaea Moon
Problems in Annady's Core

May Your Heart Be Light
We Can't Let You In, A Diary of the PyreDees Plague of 2016
She's Not Broken, IMADJINN 2019 Best Literary Fiction Novel
How to Train Your Human: A Guide for Parrots
Move the Stars

"A Legacy Protected," *Winter's Night, Vol I*
"Desecrated Ring," Keith Publications Halloween
"Dragons in Crisis," *Winter's Night, Vol II*
"Perceptions on New Year's Eve," *A Yuletide Wish* Anthology
"Woman Off the Grid," *Wild Women* Anthology
2020 Pushcart Prize Nominee, IMADJINN 2020 Short Story Finalist
"Della Finds Her Gift," TulipTree Genre Anthology

Visit **www.SandyLenderInk.com**
Problems in Annady's Core
First edition copyright 2020

Dedication

To all my dragons...

Acknowledgments

Once upon a time, Crystal and Sally contributed to a GoFundMe account set up for the purpose of marketing expenses. In exchange for their gracious support, they get to be terraformers on the Planet Annady. It's not a huge payoff in their favor, all things considered, but I tried to write meaningful roles for them.

The list of people I am grateful for is long, but for this book, I'll put Crystal and Sally at the top. I also thank Stephen Zimmer for his editing help and counsel.

Finally, a big thank-you goes out to the other writers who participate in The International 3-Day Novel Contest and who offer moral support back and forth throughout the year.

Cast of Characters

Main

Khiry Okerson — 17-year-old spaceship captain of the Coronado

Kor (John Ashley McCormick III) — 19-year-old marksman of the Coronado

Electra Endh — 16-year-old sister of El Presidente Lamahl Endh and the Coronado's communications liaison to United Society for Peace and Strength (USPS)

Onyx — adult dragon from Eldora Moon (black as night and regal)

Supporting (in order of appearance/mention)

Lacy Smith — daughter of Patient Zero in the Pangaea Moon plague, 10-year-old girl now traveling with the crew

Devin Alderman — 39-year-old doctor aboard the Coronado

Mongoose — 17-year-old security chief for the Coronado

Frederick — engineer from the Eleos who came aboard as a pilot while the crew was recently docked on Earth

Maubry — 16-year-old chief engineer of the Coronado, Panger System alien

El Presidente Lamahl Endh — Electra's older brother, president of Earth's United Society for Peace and Strength (USPS)

Jevron — a new security officer Mongoose hired on Earth

Max Sausen — 39-year-old doctor, friend of Devin Alderman, joined the crew while above Pangaea Moon

Adam Okerson — Khiry's older brother, joined the crew while above Pangaea Moon

Governor Arbaseys Laino — leader of the main colony on Annady

Tempel Pliny — librarian/historian and member of the Annady Council

Sally Cobbler — medical practitioner and a member of the Annady Council

Cassidy Hopely — communications officer and a member of the Annady Council

Donna — a young mixling on Annady, Governor Laino's favorite

Justin Dreary — a guard among the colonists of Annady's main colony

Holly Phimmer — a chef of the Coronado, joined the crew on Earth

Trilby — a young mixling on Annady

Daniel Heart — leader at the second colony on Annady

Dexter — a guard at the second colony on Annady

Jillian — a young mixling on Annady

Crystal — a doctor at the second colony on Annady

The Dragons

Junior — young dragon from Eldora Moon (reddish-brown and cute)

Nellie — adult dragon from Pangaea Moon

Goldie — a phoenix (small dragon) from Annady, friend to Trilby

Hera — a phoenix from Annady

Delta — a phoenix from Annady, friend to Jillian

Short Story from the Coronado's Bibliotecha

Bay of Naples, Earth, 79 A.D.

Arbaseys sneered through haze and steam at pebbles raining down on his city. He sneered because he didn't believe in the lies his neighbors did. He didn't believe the gods had sent a rocky pestilence to destroy them.

For days, his neighbors had whined about how long it had taken to build their temples, blaming one another for the choking dust and debris. They'd cried out as if prayers to false gods could stop the shaking of the mountain five miles away.

This new hail of pumice was one more strange sign on a strange day. It was as ominous as the darkening of the afternoon sun when the cloud of ash began climbing ever higher from the cap of the mountain he watched from his balcony.

At his feet, three steps inside the stone room, his son Matteo lay dead from the debauchery of the city's games. The lad's thick brown hair draped across his face, hiding dark eyes that closed mere hours before everyone else's eyes would close this day.

Beside Matteo, the slave girl Caledonna fell to her knees, weeping. Her upper body covering Matteo's, her tears washed his face. Apparently, she saw no point in hiding her feelings from the master of the house; Matteo could no longer protect her from any of the family.

"Take her to my brothel. Put her to work," Arbaseys commanded someone she couldn't see. Between the darkness that had descended when Mount Vesuvius belched earlier that day and the tears smearing her vision now, Caledonna watched the blue and bloody colors of Matteo's tunic blur as men's hands lifted her away.

Whether she believed in a pantheon of higher beings to protect her from the master's sick business or not, Caledonna would be spared from a life of prostitution. The city she'd been brought to as a child would be judged that day and night by nature itself. The horrible man she'd been forced to call master as she carried pitchers of wine around his grand stone home would gasp for air as he died in agony.

His demise came within three hours of Matteo's death.

In the final explosion of pyroclastic from the mountain, Master Arbaseys drew one breath of noxious, superheated gases and ash that caused liquid to fill his lungs. His second breath mixed the fluid with cinders to create goopy, foaming lava in his lungs and windpipe. His final attempt to gasp for breath thickened the lava into throat-clogging cement.

Suffocation followed.

Within twenty-four hours, every heathen in Pompeii had died and entered a state of preservation beneath four or more meters of packed sediment.

CHAPTER ONE

Khiry Okerson had no memory of the no-wake zones that existed before exponential sea level rise (EXSLR) eradicated most of the seaports on Earth. Her late father, Abraham Okerson, had compared the no-hyperdrive zones within solar systems to them, so she understood the concept. With her crewmembers gently maneuvering the Coronado toward the rim of Earth's solar system, she felt confident in their non-disruptive skills, and went to lie down in her quarters.

She couldn't remember the last time she'd been able to relax. Sure, she'd spent plenty of time lying on an uncomfortable cot while in the Wascana on Earth, but that was hardly what you'd call relaxing. Khiry looked forward to an hour, maybe two, of deep sleep. The kind where your whole body stayed in one, motionless lump on a foam board, while your brain shut down all nonessential functions.

It would be glorious.

Captain's quarters were adjacent the bridge; she moved toward that goal when Electra's voice over the intercom summoned her there more quickly. "Captain, incoming message for you on the bridge."

Khiry had just stepped into the gray cargo hold and waggled her fingers in greeting at Lacy Smith. Thank God the girl had good days like this when she could play and be a child; she could pretend she had a normal childhood unfolding aboard a spaceship roaming the galaxies without her parents.

Lacy, aged ten, wore red ponytails asymmetrically scattered around her head, and currently sported an outrageously puffy blue and silver princess dress, complete with sequins reflecting prisms off the cargo hold's security lights. She hunched down behind a wooden crate. No doubt she'd snag the net underskirt on a splintered corner of the crate with her antics. It was in danger of a tear when she lifted the taffeta material to hop to her left, executing a fabulous twirl to swirl her back against a taller box that looked even more splintered. With a handful of blue skirt wadded up in her hand, she exposed shimmery blue jeggings and black steel-toed boots.

On the other side of the box, a reddish-brown dragon about the size of a tween slunk toward the front of the hold like a cat.

A cat possibly intoxicated with catnip.

Junior couldn't be called a graceful dragon yet.

Khiry quickened her pace past this game among the crates to a set of wide metal steps leading to the bridge in the forward section of the ship. As she clomped to the top, another voice—this one a man's—shouted over the intercom, "Captain! Need you in the infirmary posthaste." The intercom clicked off the sound of someone shouting in the background.

Khiry turned and pointed at the ten-year-old below: "Lacy, take Junior to your quarters, please. Sounds like trouble."

"Yes, Captain."

No hesitation. Good girl.

As Khiry bounded onto the bridge, she asked the four crewmembers assembled there, "What's going on?"

Her doe-brown eyes adjusted quickly to the Coronado's dim helm. As always. She was meant to be its captain and companion, even if the darkness of space made the bubble of the bridge mysterious around her. "I need to get to sick bay. Can this message wai…"

When she looked from Electra's exotic features to the bulbous window where space and stars and a sharp-looking warship matched their no-hyperdrive-zone speed, her heart rate shot up a dozen beats per minute. Ferocious gun turrets pointed from black-as-night panels toward the Coronado as if already threatening the cargo vessel with mere presence.

"Whoa."

It took her the pause of a breath to gather her thoughts. "Okay." She pointed at Mongoose, the security chief. "Would you go to sick bay and deal with what's happening there? Report to me."

"On it." The blonde wall of power grabbed a plasma gun from the freestanding console in front of her before skipping out.

Next, Khiry turned to Kor at the weapons station. "Where are we?"

"Almost at Neptune."

She processed that. They could probably get away with hitting hyperdrive if they needed to run. Then, a scary thought occurred to her. "Oh, crap! Where's Pluto?"

"*Not* inside Neptune's orbit," Kor said. Khiry could hear the amusement in his voice without looking at him. "We're safe," he added.

After working together for over two years, he could obviously read her mind. At least, he knew she didn't want to accidently slam into a dwarf planet. Or anything else in the Kuiper Belt.

"Okay, let's open a channel," Khiry told Electra.

The communications liaison pushed three buttons in sequence on her control station. Khiry approached so she could be in front of the camera if necessary.

"This is Captain Okerson of the Coronado. May I be of assistance?"

An officer in another ship's uniform colors filled the console screen where Khiry and Electra focused their attention.

"That's quaint, little girl. We're here to board and take command of the Coronado. Slow to atmosphere speed and we'll come alongside."

Khiry closed her eyes, leaning one hand on the back of Electra's chair. "Say that again, please? It sounded like you wanted us to slow to atmo speed for boarding?"

"They closed the channel," Electra said.

"Should I slow down?" a young man asked.

Khiry opened her eyes to glower at the lad someone had hired as a pilot while she and Electra were in the Godforsaken Wascana on Earth. "What? No. No, we don't slow down to be boarded by some strange ship of cretins while we're on a mission for El Presidente. What's your name?"

"Frederick," he whined through wiry lips.

"Frederick, look, I don't mean to snap at you. But this crew has been through worse than a group of marauders threatening to board us. We can outrun that ship. We have more efficient engines than it does."

The kid nodded as if he forgave her for being short with him, but Khiry felt as if she'd done something rude.

"We'll get out of this," Khiry said, still trying to be polite. "Electra, is the Eleos still in the system? Can you hail them for help? Two against one will be better odds."

Time seemed to slow for all of them while Electra's slender fingers glided across the panel before her, like a pianist performing an etude. The young lady displayed grace in all she did, even with the pressure of a warship looming off the starboard bow.

The Eleos that Khiry thought of had been on the loading pad back on Earth. When they had approached the dockyards, the Eleos had caught Khiry's eye because it was the same cargo class as the Coronado.

She knew its mission took it far from any outpost the Coronado—or any other ship—would encounter, but they all had to exit the Solar System via the same trajectory if they were following United Society for Peace and Strength (USPS) codes and regs.

* * * * *

As was customary for USPS-regulated dockyards on Earth, the spaceships had been lined up in one long row with the most important — the one that had carried the president's sister — closest to the terminal. That made the travel to government buildings offsite take longer for the important people, but effectively put the important people on display for all the other ships. Other captains and mercs could see emissaries come and go, if they were paying attention.

The Coronado had the beautiful Electra Endh aboard, which meant the Coronado received special treatment. Giving her a sense of pride, the prime placement had also given Khiry a chance to see all the other ships as an official USPS hovercraft carried her, Electra, Mongoose, and some overstuffed USPS guard, smoothly along the airport side road toward the terminal, toward the airport, and toward her crew.

Her bruised and odd-looking cargo ship had been given priority in front of the shiny transport vessels and food supply ships for the terraformers. She'd held her chin up a little higher as she climbed off the hovercraft next to the moving sidewalk that would carry her to the source of her pride.

The bruises on her ship matched the wounds she carried.

They were signs of strength.

Of history.

Of survival.

The other ship built similarly to the Coronado wasn't as beat up. No dents from torpedo hits scarred the Eleos' shiny surface.

So far.

The battleship gray of the Eleos' surface served the purpose of fading into the horizon like memory, which would benefit the ship's crew while within a planet's atmosphere.

Khiry preferred the dark, gunmetal gray of her ship, which blended into the empty black of deep space. She'd even taken her engineer Maubry's advice to affix mirrors strategically around the hull to reflect star patterns. Her Coronado could slide into nothingness with a mere whisper of propulsion and no one could find her.

While sitting on the ground, both ships had the fluid feel of seamless panels built for clean re-entry. Both had the bulbous front end where the bridge seemed to have been tacked on after the rest of the ship had been built.

The bridge sat there like a misshapen bubble of metal and windows slapped into place on the front of a fat-winged submarine. Two ion-controlled engines stuck out like globs to port and starboard, and water-electrolysis-based engines extended like three Spanish Christmas ornaments on the back. The ships boasted a great deal of width in their mid-sections, lending an air of mechanical obesity to each one.

"Look at all that rice," Electra had said.

Khiry had shifted her focus from the metal of spaceships to the marshes of food far beyond the airfield. She hadn't been to South Saskatchewan before leaving Earth with her family a decade before.

During her education in the schools in what was left of the United States or aboard her family's cargo ship, she'd not learned much about what was left of Canada or the changes it had gone through since the sea level rise had started its upward curve—since EXSLR had driven governments to bold and expensive action.

It made sense that the areas where prairies had grown in the past would give way to marshes, cotton fields, and rice paddies, but she thought Regina and its surroundings had been filled up with skyscrapers and the hustle and bustle of any provincial capital city. Had these places been knocked down in favor of food production?

"It's probably more important to have rice growing there than housing," Mongoose had mused, as if echoing Khiry's thoughts.

"I saw a report while we were in the Wascana that new housing is finished that juts out over the southern area where Central America used to be," Electra had said. "Llama approved the permits a few years ago and the teams got it built in record time. It's anchored down at Chirripo Grande in Costa Rica, a couple of the high points in Honduras, and Tajumulco in Guatemala."

Khiry had picked up their conversation at the mention of the mountains. "Tajumulco?"

"Yes."

"Isn't that a volcano?" Khiry had asked.

"Yeah, it is," Mongoose had answered. "How stupid is that?"

"Tajumulco is not an active volcano," their escort had interjected.

It was the first thing the officer in USPS gray had said since they'd left the hospital. All three of the young women had looked back at Officer Ovos, holding the string of a duffel bag as if holding a fine China teacup. Pinky extended.

Khiry had found that odd. If the bag's weight shifted, the soldier's tenuous hold on the string wasn't going to prevent it from sliding off the conveyor. He'd have to hop off the people-mover to collect it.

"You mean it's not active right now," Mongoose had corrected him.

"There's no reason to believe it will erupt in the next few thousand years," he had said, as if offended. "The government studied it before building one of the stanchions upon it."

Mongoose had shaken her head slightly, looking down at the moving sidewalk carrying them to a slow stop near the Coronado's loading pad. It had been apparent she didn't agree, but she wouldn't argue some insignificant point. "I sure don't think I'd trust geologists at this point in history."

"Volcanologists," their escort had corrected.

"Them either." Mongoose had reached for the duffel bag as she continued, "Want me to get that for—"

"I will assist you," Officer Ovos had snapped.

Khiry had rethought her assessment of the soldier's ability to catch the bag should it shift or fall. The man's fast reflexes had collected the bag off the conveyor in the blink of an eye. Had he been chivalrous, keeping the weight of the duffel bag for him rather than letting the seventeen-year-old girl carry it? Or had he brought some sort of problem to their ship?

Mongoose had eyed the soldier coolly. "Of course. Are we taking on that cargo?"

"This is medical supplies for your crew specifically," Officer Ovos had said.

* * * * *

"The Eleos isn't responding," Electra's sultry voice interrupted Khiry's reminiscing. "She's gone."

"Open a link to sick bay, please," Khiry said.

To her credit, Electra didn't question the captain's change in interest from the warship awaiting their answer to the problem on board. She pressed the appropriate button to open a comm link to Doctor Alderman's domain and said, "Devin?"

"Where's the captain?" a frantic male voice asked from the console speaker. A solid thwack in the background startled everyone on the bridge.

"Mongoose is on her way," Khiry supplied. "Did Officer Ovos stow away?"

"No. That blasted bag of his did. Spiders. They're multiplying or something."

Khiry shuddered involuntarily. "Spang them, Doc."

Another slap sound answered before the man did. "Working on that. I think some got out of sick bay."

Khiry and Electra exchanged looks of disgust before Khiry reached for a toggle that swooshed the bridge door closed on its track. She heard Kor chuckle from his station a few feet away. She chose to ignore him.

"Captain, they're huge."

Another thwack.

"Define huge," Khiry said.

"The body's bigger than my hand."

Khiry shuddered again.

Before she could respond, the doctor continued. "They hurt when they bite. The fangs are at least an inch long. I advise confining everyone to quarters. Mongoose!"

"Mongoose, Devin, I need you to control the spider problem," Khiry said. "We have unfriendlies in the sky."

"On it," Mongoose's voice answered. "Over and out."

Khiry looked to the new pilot, Frederick. "We're gonna punch this thing into space. What's your experience?"

"I worked on the Eleos. In engineering."

Khiry didn't stop to consider how the weaselly lad could have worked in the engineering section of a vessel as important as the Eleos; she had other mysteries to solve. "And she's already left the system, you say, El?"

"I don't know about that," Kor said. "I've got some readings over here." The marksman worked knobs at his station while he spoke. "I'm sorry to break the news like this, but I think the Eleos was destroyed."

Frederick gasped. Then, he lurched toward the floor as a sizable chunk of shrapnel hit the ship.

Something nearby had exploded.

Something large sent debris on a trajectory that caught them off guard.

CHAPTER TWO

"Did they just *fire* at us?" Electra asked. Her typically sultry voice took on an edge of anger, as if she were offended.

"That was something farther away," Kor said, flipping a plexiglass covering open on the panel in front of him. "Radiation coming off it is way low."

Khiry agreed with him but wasn't taking time to explain why. The Okerson family business transporting "goods" had put her in a position to be far too familiar with high-speed debris and widespread radiation aftereffects of explosions in space. She hobbled to the helmsman post while the ship rocked back to equilibrium.

"Umm, the Telkines is coming about," Frederick whined.

"Stay down," Kor ordered him.

Khiry had faith in her marksman. She left him to his job while she punched buttons and opened a channel to engineering. "Maubry!"

"Here, Captain. What was—"

"I need hyperdrive right now," she barked.

"Yes, Captain." Pause. "Give me. One. Second."

Electra hit the intercom to the whole ship: "All hands. We're entering hyperdrive. Grab hold of something."

Maubry's voice continued to emanate from Khiry's station. "You have mix in three. Two. Now!"

Kor fired at the warship.

Khiry punched the button for mix in the engines. The Coronado whined for half a second before jumping into fast forward. Frederick grabbed the leg of the helmsman station to prevent being flung to the back of the bridge. Quick as a flash, they left the Solar System for deep space.

It took another second or two to swallow and clear their ears, as if bringing themselves to equilibrium with the ship's new reality. Electra leaned over to help Frederick to his chair, and Khiry braced against the side of the helmsman console. "This isn't very dry," she muttered.

"What exactly did we get signed up for?" Kor asked.

Khiry shook her head. "Something that should clear our name of any problems from our past. Helping Pangaea Moon shouldn't come with a side of warship-firing-on-us before we even get out of the Solar System."

"I agree," Electra said. "It doesn't make sense that the Telkines, or any ship, would try to stop us from going back to Pangaea Moon. Llama personally asked us to go there."

While Electra described what her brother had asked of her, Khiry did a quick internal review of her incarceration on Earth. What had they missed? What should she have picked up on, to explain a warship coming after them?

If not for backstabbing family members, she and the crew of the Coronado would have been cruising through space to deliver supplies to help recovery efforts on Pangaea Moon a fortnight earlier. Instead, she and Electra had been detained in South Saskatchewan for seven days.

Mere hours before staring at the imposing warship in space, Khiry had been lying on an uncomfortable cot, trying to tell her friend that her presidential brother was their enemy without offending her.

Khiry wouldn't lie to Electra, but she couldn't tell her outright that she didn't trust Electra's brother, either. Of course, the fancy presidential brother seemed to have been the one keeping them in prison at the time.

Distrust might have been easy to explain.

El Presidente Lamahl Endh himself had requested an audience with his younger sister on their home planet. He'd made the request while she and her captain friend were in the midst of a whacky plan to heal the people of Pangaea Moon from a zombie plague.

What were the chances she'd live through that? What were the chances the crew would be successful and make it to Earth for the meet-up? He could have invited Electra home without expecting her to make it.

Taking Presidente Endh at his word and accepting the olive branch had resulted in Khiry and Electra going through a series of interviews with doctors, psychiatrists, world ministers, and the leader himself. Then, they'd landed in a containment ward at the refurbished Wascana Rehabilitation Centre in Regina, Saskatchewan, where the bibliotheca screens showed detainees only what the USPS officials wanted them to see.

The news had said nothing about dreadnoughts bebopping around the Solar System preventing El Presidente's missions of peace and aid.

*   *   *   *   *

Two hours after the jump into hyperdrive and away from the warship, the crewmembers had returned to their tasks, including the job of killing spiders. The Coronado hurtled through space at a frightening clip for Frederick; it was nothing to the teens who had been shooting between the stars for months. The familiar whir of the engines soothed at least some of Khiry's nerves as she moved through the cargo bay.

"There are too many people on this ship," Khiry muttered, taking the metal steps to the bridge two at a time. Mongoose followed her. They met Kor at the platform at the top. He looked over the cargo hold, where Mongoose's new security hire, Jevron, used a kitchen knife from the galley to kill what spiders he didn't kill by stomping.

"I'd say there are too many spiders," Mongoose muttered back.

Kor pushed forward his lower lip, as if considering this. "It might not be manly to say it, but the spiders are starting to creep me out."

"Devin says they're not poisonous," Khiry offered.

"Then why are they here?" Mongoose asked. "Why did Ovos put them aboard?"

"They're a distraction," Kor said.

Khiry agreed with that. The eight-legged creatures were distracting. They multiplied faster than they died, shivering out of their exoskeletons into a trio of arachnids where there had only been one, like some kind of eight-legged cellular mitosis. The ship would be overrun before they could land anywhere.

"They're spinning webs in the galley," he continued. "Soon, we won't be able to get in there."

"Are they supposed to starve us?" Mongoose asked.

Khiry shook her head. "I don't think it's starvation Ovos was after. Just distraction. This will make us stop before we get to Pangaea. We'll infest someplace between Earth and Pangaea with these things. Our mission will fail. Endh will look foolish for sending us on the errand. Something political is behind this."

Kor met her eyes. "You sound like a conspiracy theorist all of a sudden."

"Probably because I had contact with my father so recently," she murmured.

She was certain Kor would have smiled and offered some reassuring comment if they weren't being overrun by arachnids and chased by a dreadnought.

"Speaking of fathers, Frederick's kind of a mess up there," Kor said. "He's staying at his post, but…"

"Were his parents on the Eleos?" Khiry asked.

"His dad was. Not sure about his mom."

Khiry frowned. "That's a shame."

She looked back at the cargo hold where a sleek black dragon had joined the fight to regain control. The familiar surge of pride swelled inside her. This magnificent beast aboard her ship was her friend, working to help restore order at her behest.

She had named the creature Onyx because each black scale shone as if etched by a sculptor's perfect hand. She had told the dragon that he was as beautiful as the onyx stone made from chalcedony on Earth. Men carved it into vases and cameos that still sold for thousands of dollars. It awed her that the creature of such beauty and strength had stayed aboard the ship as her companion.

While she watched him crunch spiders beneath his enormous feet and squeeze them in his foreclaws, her pride smoothed into something less arrogant. She felt less pride and more gratitude.

She turned to Kor, to offer the reassuring smile she had anticipated from him. "I'll talk to Frederick. He's a brave kid to stay at his post despite the grief he's got to be feeling. Will you help with the spider problem while Mongoose fills me in on what happened on Earth? If the Telkines catches up with us, I'll make sure Electra lets you know."

"Sounds like a good plan. I'd rather El not mess with the weapons." He winked at her. "Or you."

As she moved toward the bridge, Khiry wondered at that comment. Why should he wish to keep her from using the weapons? She'd proved herself proficient with any number of them. Of course, Mongoose was their security chief and Kor the marksman, which meant the captain of the ship didn't *have* to take up arms, but situations had called for it plenty of times since Captain Marlon of the Instigator had committed treason against USPS and put the crew in harm's way.

Khiry thought she'd done a fine job of stepping up in light of all that had happened. It stung to think otherwise.

She had to remind herself of the positive feelings Onyx had instilled in her just a few moments before as she stepped over the threshold of the bridge and saw Frederick staring blankly at the dark window of space in front of him. The young man appeared to be struggling with his emotions, because his eyes brimmed with tears.

She swallowed an imagined lump of empathy in her throat and took a seat at Kor's weapons station. Mongoose stopped to lean against the bulkhead at the back of the bridge, waiting for a spider to dare enter this domain. Electra offered a calm presence for them all — the graceful and gentle young woman who could broker peace with a mere gesture.

No wonder El Presidente sent us on this mission to the Panger System, Khiry thought. *We're a good team for it.*

"I want to extend my sympathies for what happened earlier," Khiry told Frederick. She surprised herself with the calm that filled her voice, with the calm that settled over the bridge when she spoke. It was pleasing.

"Thank you," he murmured. When he blinked, a tear spilled from each eye.

"Kor tells me you may have had family aboard the Eleos."

Silence.

"I'm sure you had friends among the colleagues you lost today," she prodded softly.

This time, he nodded and met her gaze. "I didn't get to say goodbye to all of them before the Eleos had to launch. I came aboard before I got messages to everyone."

"That must be difficult to think about."

"Yeah. I wanna think some of my friends didn't even know I was gone. I mean…" His voice trailed away, and the three officers let him think of what he wanted to tell them. They watched his beady eyes seeking a point on the bridge where they could stare, somewhere that wasn't Khiry's face.

"I mean some of my friends were in parts of the ship I didn't work in, so they didn't know I'd transferred. So, they died without knowing I abandoned them to die."

"You didn't abandon them to die," Khiry offered. "You can't think that way or it'll drive you nuts. No one could have guessed that—"

He already shook his head as he interrupted her, his head wobbling atop a skinny neck. "But I knew."

Khiry's pulse skipped for part of a second. "What do you mean? What did you know?"

"I knew USPS'd never let them carry out their mission."

"And what was that?" Khiry asked.

"To go to Annady and help the terraformers there."

"Okay. Umm, why do you think a world government would send a whole ship full of people on a mission and then try to stop them?"

"For the same reason they sent the Telkines to stop you from going to Pangaea Moon." He referenced the dreadnought as if he had great familiarity with it. "But I didn't know they wanted to stop your mission, too, or I wouldn't've come along. I wouldn't've boarded." He paused, as if deciding how much he wanted to reveal, before plunging into his confession.

"I'm a coward," he hiccupped. "I know there're resistance members who wanna stop USPS from colonizing *any* other planets. And there are USPS members who wanna overthrow El Presidente."

As he spoke, his voice rose in pitch, and his pace took on more urgency. Khiry sat back a bit in the chair at the weapons station while she absorbed the growing energy from the young man. She expected spittle to form at the edges of his thin, wiry lips, and there was no point in being too close to that.

"And there are people everywhere who have these secret agendas to keep us from terraforming *anywhere* outside of our galaxy. They'll destroy any ship they can, but I didn't think they'd come after Coronado because Electra Endh is here. I thought there'd at least be *some* respect for her, coz no one knows whose side she's on, yet she can offer power to whichever side she chooses to be on.

"The captain of Eleos was s'posed to go to Annady to help those people because the resistance wanted it done and the government was conceding to that as a peace offering despite the mixlings they're rumored to have there. But I knew USPS would stop it.

"And Coronado is going to the Panger System, which can only mean you're going back to Pangaea Moon to help those people with the disease outbreak. Everyone's heard about the outbreak there, and no one wants it to get back to Earth, but I thought you'd be safe to at least get there because of Electra—"

"Okay, Frederick, calm down. Relax. You're very upset. We're not gonna die out here. We *are* going to Pangaea Moon and we'll make it just fine."

"But the Telkines is coming for you!"

Khiry offered the lad her most comforting smile. "We've been through rougher stuff than some warship that can't even catch up to us in space."

The crazed look he leveled on her sent a shudder up her spine. His eyes went wider than they had during his rant about governments and resistances. His already thin lips went taut, peeling back from his teeth and he hissed from behind them: "The captain of the Telkines believes in his cause. He won't stop until he kills every last one of you."

Khiry didn't like the way Frederick left himself out of that threat. It occurred to her that he might be working for two masters. Maybe he was acting as a spy or double agent who had joined her crew to sabotage them. "El," Khiry asked, "are we broadcasting anything?"

"Well, that's not gonna be dry," Electra muttered.

CHAPTER THREE

The bridge of the Coronado hosted senior staff meetings more often than any other portion of the ship. Khiry liked the bulbous windows to the universe as a backdrop to their important discussions — as if stars in the heavens offered the right reminder that they held more than their own lives in their hands when they made decisions in this dimly blue room.

Of course, none of the crewmembers thought of their meetups as "meetings" *per se*. Typically, if Khiry needed to ask Devin, Maubry, and Mongoose to join her, Electra, and Kor on the bridge, it wasn't a meeting. It was probably life-hangs-in-the-balance-while-officers-of-USPS-Authority-Customs-Service-stare-down-a-plasma-canon-at-us.

With Frederick locked in the brig, Khiry asked her senior staff to join her on the bridge to discuss their situation.

- John Ashley McCormick III (Kor) served as the ship's marksman and hadn't joined the meeting yet.
- Maubry, the chief engineer, leaned against the helmsman station so he could be close to Mongoose.
- Misty Argoln (Mongoose), the security chief, filled in as pilot for the moment, as she'd been practicing after their events above Pangaea Moon.
- Electra Endh, the communications liaison, sat at her station full of blue, red, green, and orange buttons and toggles.
- Devin Alderman, the ship's doctor and oldest member of the senior crew at thirty-nine years of age, sat on the floor, as if to remind everyone of his flexibility.

Onyx the dragon sat on the floor next to the doctor, effectively blocking a large portion of the soft tracked lighting and casting that section of the bridge in a deep shadow. The dragon hung out with them, not because he was part of the senior staff, but because he tended to understand when his favorite human had something important happening. He now watched that favorite human, Khiry Okerson, pacing back and forth while waiting for Kor to join the group in the crowded bridge space.

Electra motioned with a slender finger in Khiry's direction when the captain turned on her bootheel away from the front windows. "I found the signal's origin," Electra said. "I can piggyback our own message on it when we're ready."

"Okay," Khiry breathed, the implication of gratitude in the word.

"Spider detail is in Dr. Max's capable hands," Kor announced, as he stepped onto the bridge. "Shall I close this door?" He offered a sly glance at Khiry, as if his suggestion was for her amusement.

She pretended not to notice his teasing, and simply answered, "For the best."

With the press of a button, Kor sealed them in the blue space with their dark business.

"I have a question to put to you all," Khiry said. "This isn't a decision I want to make for anyone else."

She took a deep breath before continuing.

"Here's the situation. Some of you met Frederick, the kid piloting the ship earlier."

Kor took his seat at the weapons station, swiveling to watch his captain pace. A couple people nodded in response to Khiry.

"He served aboard the Eleos before trying out with us," Khiry continued. "An agent aboard the Telkines got to him and pumped him for information about the Eleos' mission to Annady. Before we entered hyperdrive earlier, the Telkines destroyed the Eleos and came after us. Frederick thinks the captain of the Telkines wants to divert our mission from Pangaea Moon. The Telkines captain may or may not wish to destroy our ship with all hands aboard. He might want to abduct Electra Endh first."

Electra gave a weak, princess wave, as if anyone on the bridge didn't know her and hadn't served with her for the past couple of months.

"Frederick has put a subspace beacon out so the Telkines can follow us wherever we go," Khiry said. She didn't stop to acknowledge the gasp from Maubry. "Of course, we can disengage it, but we may choose to send a message back to the Telkines. Or we can set up a decoy for them."

"I like that," Devin interrupted. "A decoy."

"Then we lose track of where they are," Kor said.

Khiry pointed at Kor. "Exactly. So, I put it to you guys. Do we send them a decoy that leads them to a trap? Do we destroy the Telkines with all hands aboard before they destroy us?"

"Whoa," Devin said. "You don't mean to kill all those people?"

No one spoke for a moment. Khiry listened to the hum of her ship's voice, considering whether or not she could destroy another vessel without harming the people aboard. Could she get the people off of it first?

"They killed all the people on the Eleos," Maubry pointed out. "And wasn't the Eleos setting out on a mission to help the people of Annady? A mission of peace? They didn't deserve to be murdered when they were on a mission of peace."

"Correct," Khiry said. "But that wasn't any of our business. I'm not suggesting we take it upon ourselves to exact revenge. We aren't the self-appointed judge and jury out here in space. I'm talking about what we want to do to protect ourselves."

"Can we disable them without destroying their ship?" Electra asked.

"Possible," Kor answered. "I can target anything. Execution is another matter."

Devin responded, "Then the question becomes, are we going to disable a ship and leave the people aboard floating in space to die a slow death, or are we going to kill them outright and be the instant instrument of their deaths?"

Khiry put a hand to her temple.

"We don't know that disabling their ship would condemn them to death," Maubry said.

"Leaving people to drift in space is not entirely compassionate," Devin said.

"El's not suggesting we take out their life support," Kor said.

"Didn't the people on that ship show no such mercy to the Eleos?" Mongoose asked.

"That only means they deserve to be put on trial," the doctor argued. "They don't necessarily deserve to be executed in the cold of space."

"This," Khiry announced, getting everyone's attention back on herself. "This is why I wished to have you all visit with me about the decision before us. We've worked together to save lives from a zombie plague. We can figure out what we do in this situation. And let's come up with some constructive ideas quickly because the Telkines isn't stopping to have tea and crumpets somewhere while we chat."

"Tea and crumpets?" Maubry asked under his breath.

Mongoose spoke just as quietly, "It's an old Earth expression."

"Here's a question," Devin said. "Does the Telkines know we're going to Pangaea Moon?"

"Frederick says yes," Khiry said.

"Then should we continue in that direction?" Maubry asked, picking up on the doctor's idea. "Or should we abort the mission?"

Khiry hadn't thought of that. She looked to Electra for her reaction.

The exotic young lady shrugged her shoulders. "I hadn't thought of that."

"The people on Pangaea Moon are waiting for the supplies we have," Kor said.

"What supplies did we take on for them? I was in the Wascana with her," Khiry nodded toward Electra, "when you guys got the order to take us there."

"It's mostly parts to fix equipment like their fans and air filters," Maubry said. "I recognize a lot of it. Then, of course, medical stuff. A lot of antibiotics, for some reason. But lots of face masks. Lots. Boxes of cartons full of face masks."

"Yes, Max and I sorted medicines and supplies for the hospitals," Devin said.

"We've taken on the basics that Pangaea needs," Khiry said absently, as if summarizing out loud what she learned. Her mind tossed around the idea that USPS authorities still thought the plague on Pangaea Moon required face masks to prevent its spread.

"Any ship could take these things to the Panger System," Maubry said.

"You're thinking we take up the Eleos' mission," Devin said.

"But Annady is nowhere near Pangaea Moon," Maubry continued.

"Annady is nowhere near anything," Mongoose said.

They all considered the implications for a moment. The planet of Annady posed a number of problems for terraforming due to its remoteness. The atmosphere and landscape had been reasonable enough for USPS officers to put notices on all the bibliotecha channels that earthlings were needed for a terraforming colony there.

Twenty-some-odd years later, the government hadn't bothered to engineer a solution to the communication barriers between Annady and Earth. Or between Annady and any of the outposts earthlings monitored.

The problem? A wide, curved cluster of space debris hung like some kind of cosmic net amid a set of planets — none of which were good candidates for terraforming — within a lightyear of Annady, effectively forming a barrier in space that ships had to navigate around.

If approaching Annady on a trajectory that started at Earth—or any of the currently inhabited planets or moons—a ship would be forced to go around a convex wall of asteroids, stardust, mini-moons, and "hanging" starnets. The field of debris was dense enough, and comprised of magnetic enough materials, that typical communication signals couldn't penetrate it.

The colony on Annady had to send missives to a satellite many lightyears away, bounce them to another satellite, and so on, to get around the wall. It made Annady's seclusion almost complete.

"Going through the panel is like going through the Bermuda Triangle," Maubry warned. The pangering's deep voice lent an air of foreboding to the already moody statement.

Kor puzzled over his comment. While Kor agreed with the engineer's allegory, he scratched the stubble on his chin. How could he politely ask: *Why is a pangering making references to such an old Earth myth?* Now that Puerto Rico—which housed one of the three apexes of the triangle—had been submerged by sea level rise after devastating earthquakes had shaken the island apart, the concept of the Devil's Triangle had kind of gone by the wayside, and seafarers of Earth had given up blaming Sirens and ghosts for their Caribbean misfortunes.

Khiry watched her marksman frowning over Maubry's Bermuda Triangle analogy and wanted to bring up the complications of trying to reach the colony when she spoke again. "I believe it would be in our best interest to cripple the Telkines so badly that she has to stop somewhere. Changing our destination would be smart in case they signal for backup or send a second ship after us."

"You think they're not alone," Electra said.

"I think only the paranoid survive," Khiry answered.

"It's best to be prepared," Kor agreed.

"If they're acting on orders from some level of the resistance, how many ships can we reasonably expect them to have?" Khiry asked. "I mean, how well-funded is the resistance on Earth? Do we know the size of its armada at this point?"

"If they're acting on orders from the government, they're not going to survive their mission anyway," Mongoose said.

"That's morbid," Maubry said.

"But fair to think," Mongoose continued. "The government doesn't send a crew out to destroy a couple of ships and leave witnesses behind."

"Neither does the resistance," Kor said.

"You're not suggesting we go ahead and kill those aboard the Telkines to save their employer the trouble?" Devin asked.

"No," Mongoose said, speaking for herself and Kor. "But I'm saying we probably don't have to worry about them coming after us. I bet we could make it look like they succeeded in their 'job' and get on with our affairs."

Khiry had paced up to Onyx and put her forehead against the dragon's massive side. She closed her eyes to consider all that her fellow officers discussed. "You're all starting to sound like Frederick. Not quite as whiny or frantic as he was, but bordering on paranoid, conspiracy theories."

"You're not paranoid if people really are out to spang you from the heavens," Mongoose said. "I'd like to come up with a plan that prevents that from happening."

"I have another idea," Khiry said.

All heads turned to face her and Onyx.

"I say we keep the killing to a minimum, of course, but let's make it look like we've been in a massive battle out here. We piggyback a message for help on the beacon Frederick set up." Khiry gestured toward Electra, as if they could all see an invisible beacon vibrating on a dangerous frequency above the communications station.

"When the Telkines arrives to either destroy or rescue our crew, they're snared in a trap *we* set," Khiry continued. "They're crippled enough to slink to the nearest port. They let their employer know that the Coronado was destroyed in whatever happened out here and we're not responsible for whatever happens to them after that. We go on to Annady to complete the mission Eleos had and lay low for a while."

"For a while is right," Maubry growled.

"How do we make it look like we've been in a massive battle?" Devin asked.

"I don't know," Khiry said. "I'm a pilot, not an old Hollywood director. That's for the engineers in the group to figure out."

"We do have a lot of spare parts on board now," Maubry offered.

"And we have a few dragons that can dent them easily," Mongoose said. "As well as a couple doctors who re-wired a torpedo back above Pangaea Moon recently."

"I like it," Kor announced. "It sounds plausible."

Khiry looked to her communications officer. "El, we need to send out a message that we've been in a firefight. Can you work on the distress call while we make some space debris?"

"Of course, I can! And let's shoot some of those spiders out the airlock while we're at it. Those things give me the creeps."

CHAPTER FOUR

Watching Maubry fire homemade space debris out the airlock was like watching a boy play a video game. He almost giggled. The glee with which he shot dragon-charred spaceship panels into the heavens belied his hard, scarred physique. Back when the crew had learned that Maubry was sixteen years old, they'd each been surprised. The marks he carried on his face, neck, and muscular arms told too many stories for a youth of merely sixteen years.

Khiry left the joyful pangering to the job of sending debris into space.

In engineering, where Maubry typically hung out, Kor and the two doctors, Devin and Max, built the net of electrodes that would capture the Telkines.

"Will you have that ready soon?" Khiry asked them.

"Someone's getting antsy," Dr. Max said.

"I'm getting nervous since we slowed to no wake," she said.

Kor glanced up from the wires he twisted together. "Like sleeping?"

She'd never thought of it that way. "You might say that. We're certainly not moving like we're up and motivated."

Devin straightened from the counter where he wrapped twisted wires with plastic casing. "Are you suggesting we're not motivated?"

She liked the teasing note in his voice. She knew the older man well enough to know he didn't flirt with her. It wasn't part of the gentleman's nature to flirt with the captain of the ship: It *was* in his nature to tease her to lighten the mood when things were too tense.

"If you gentlemen can have this ready quickly, I'll go nap on the bridge," she teased right back.

Part of her wasn't teasing. She'd been wanting a nap for hours, since before the Telkines had made its menacing appearance. Maybe some rest was finally at hand.

It gave her a sense of calm to know the three oldest members of the crew worked on the most complex part of their plan. The two doctors were each nearly forty years old. They'd been through years of formal schooling that honed their minds for critical thinking, problem solving, and the task in front of them.

As Mongoose had reminded the team, the doctors had performed surgery on a torpedo just a month prior. They'd have the electric net ready for the Telkines' engines before the warship caught up with them. She had confidence in them.

She had confidence in Kor's space experience. The marksman understood how weapons and electronics worked in zero gravity and 2.73 Kelvin temperatures. The three were a formidable team for the task. As she turned to leave engineering, she tossed a compliment over her shoulder.

"You guys truly make me feel confident in our plan."

* * * * *

The rest of the trip to Annady bordered on boring compared to the rush of being chased out of the Solar System. Tension lingered due to battling enormous spiders in spurts of activity as they found clutters of them hiding and multiplying in various rooms. Tension also hung thick around Electra's communications station where they'd shut down all beacons and subspace tracers. No one could find them through typical signals.

The ship had a long way to go around the planetary and meteor debris field that blocked electronic communication between the inhabited section of space and the outskirts they hurtled toward. They had the option of slowing to the "no-wake" sort of impulse speed that would allow them to steer through the wide and ever-shifting field, but swinging around The Debris Panel, as it was colloquially known by taggers and jumpers, was the smarter thing to do.

Maubry and Khiry worked together to quiet their engine patterns as well, changing the ion signatures to resemble bursts of space storms here, vapor clouds there. They got creative in a few places, making downright beautiful light images to rival the Northern Lights back on Earth. Maubry, as a pangering, hadn't been to see the Northern Lights in real life. Khiry, as an earthling, had seen them when she was a young child. Once a person sees such a beautiful sight, it's not easy to forget. She guided Maubry in the first colorful wall of towering greens and blues.

By the time the third cloud of ghostly pinks began taking shape, Khiry merely watched. Maubry the engineer had become Maubry the painter of gases, light, and stars.

"Ah, I name this one Misty Argoln's Dream," Maubry breathed. His typically bass voice took on an airy undertone that swirled around Khiry's head. It lifted the tiny hairs deep in her ears and tickled them with a not-quite-playful tune.

Khiry and Mongoose stood next to Maubry on the bridge as they admired the whorls of tender azur caressing magenta as it descended into pink. The colors appeared to be their own entities, hanging in the forever of space, lit by their own existence.

When Maubry breathed the words that gave the trailings of color a name, Khiry felt herself blush. She intruded here in this place where ion trails gave birth to wavelengths of light. As quietly as possible, she moved off the bridge, leaving Maubry and Mongoose to enjoy the creation alone in the quiet bubble.

As she slid the bridge door gently closed, she noticed Kor sitting on a crate at the base of the stairs below. She offered him a smile as she descended the metal steps.

"What's the news?" she asked.

"I think everything's calm aboard."

For some reason, that surprised her.

"Are you serious?"

"Jevron, the guy Mongoose picked for security, came through just a minute ago saying he's getting things under control," Kor said.

"Amazing. There's nothing I need to hurry off to deal with? Nothing's on fire somewhere? No spiders are entombing a dragon in sick bay?"

He grinned. "Well, you might avoid the galley for a few more hours."

She couldn't suppress a giggle. An honest-to-God, little-girl giggle erupted from somewhere inside her. What caused that? Nerves?

"Sorry," she said, putting a hand to her mouth.

"For what? Laughing? It suits you. I haven't heard that sound out of you in a long while. To be serious, though, there are webs in the galley. To hear you laugh again, I'll tell you they're covered in essential oil of rosemary."

She couldn't help giggling again. "No!"

"Yes. We still have vats of the stuff, you know."

He alluded to the main ingredient for their zombie-air-purification routine, which would have been used upon their return to Pangaea Moon. The essential oil of rosemary had been *essential* in healing the infected residents there. It was a good item to have on hand. She imagined it weighing down and dripping from the thick webs that the spiders seemed adept at spinning. Kor watched her thinking on this.

"Devin and Dr. Max have a couple of the guys loading the webs into crates," he said. "They're all spongy with the stuff and Devin thinks it will come in handy if we run into any zombies."

"That doctor—always thinking," Khiry said. "But why would we run into zombies on Annady?"

"I don't think we will, but it's keeping some of our crew occupied and productive while we travel. Devin says it's good for their minds."

She agreed and said so. "Smart. The distraction has become a good thing."

"Apparently. How's *your* mind? Have you stayed distracted with the ion clouds and charting a course around The Debris Panel?"

She smiled at him. "Checking on my mental state?"

"Yes," he admitted, leaning forward on the crate toward her. "I *care*."

That made her blush a bit. "You sound like Doc Alderman."

"Huh. Devin doesn't care for the same reasons I do."

She knew the color in her cheeks deepened. "You're embarrassing me."

"I can tell, Captain." He gestured at the open space on the crate next to him. "Sit down for a while with me. It's good to have a minute with you when no one's freaking out about death."

She sat beside him while he continued. They both had to reposition the weapons on their belts to accommodate the closeness, but they'd had to do that before. It wasn't difficult.

"And no one's bringing you messages about cargo or updates on transports," he continued. "No one's calling over the intercom to have you check torpedoes or find bottles of perfume oils or visit with potential ship buyers."

She grinned. "This has been a non-stop tour of duty, hasn't it?"

"Yes, it has. Yes, it has. I've watched you go through a lot of changes in the last three months. Two and a half months. Whatever it's been since we crashed on Eldora Prime."

She couldn't help the feeling of pressure that lighted upon the base of her spine at the mention of that planet. Everything that had happened on Eldora Prime had been a test of her will to survive—she had passed every test so far.

"You go through days of being distant," he said.

"I know." She didn't know what else to say to that. Kor was right. There were days when she wanted to put everything out of reach to make it easier to be in command.

"I remember a moment on Eldora Prime when you were not distant," he said softly. "I had the chance to hold you and comfort you against things you feared."

His words brought back the memory of being in an electrical shed, enclosed in the tight space awaiting either death or rescue. She'd never kissed a boy the way she'd kissed Kor in that moment. It had been enlightening and frightening all at once, and she'd been avoiding a return to the circumstances ever since.

She gulped back what she assumed was girlish fear and blurted, "You're quite a bit older than me."

He didn't laugh, but she could hear amusement in his answer. "I'm almost three years older than you in Earth years. Out here in space…" He paused, as if searching for the right words. "Out here in space, I'm not sure which one of us is the older one."

She liked that sentiment. Finding moments to sit down with this handsome young man had become increasingly more difficult as she'd found the moments increasingly more appealing since their crash on Eldora Prime. Nowadays, such rare pauses of calm and kindness brought a peacefulness to her mind, even if they brought a girlish whirl to her emotions.

She felt a tingle slowly creep up her spine, some heavy sense of ticklish fingers moving upward. Kor was right. Her age on Earth would land her in a schoolroom with a teacher preaching the importance of fractions and punctuation and career selection, while getting Kor arrested for the kiss they'd shared in the confines of Eldora Prime's electrical shed.

Out here among the stars, her age landed her in the captain's chair of a ship mixed with youth, adults, dragons, earthlings, and pangerings who just wanted to make it to the next mission without getting bit by a zombie or an ugly space spider with one-inch fangs.

"Out here in space," he continued, "I'm sure there are rules we should follow, but I'm not sure what the rules are. Maybe we can make them up as we go."

When Kor turned to look in her eyes, she felt the pleasantness of emotion wash over her. His eyes were the dark brown of sinful chocolates—the kind taggers would make millions off of in the right ports.

She lost herself staring in his eyes. It was time to stop avoiding. Time to stop running from the handsome marksman who had been at her side for two years now.

The idea made the tickle along her spine creep higher.

"Whoa!" he cried out.

He jumped up, grabbing her shoulder. In an instant, she found herself moving. In one second, she stared into the depths of handsome brown eyes. In the next second, she saw the cargo bay floor coming up to greet her.

Kor's arm held her around the waist to prevent her falling. With a thwack sound to her right, a spider's guts squished out under Kor's knife.

He helped her stand next to the crate, where one of the enormous spiders twitched in its death throes. At first, the room spun from the quick movements, but everything came into focus as she realized the species' mitosis took place as it died. The paroxysms of death led to replacement beasties.

"Crap!" she said, pulling her own knife.

She drove it into one of the forming, twitching spiders. Kor had pulled his knife from the original and stabbed it into the other newly forming one. They watched to make sure this was the end. Apparently, the newly forming arachnids weren't developed enough to set off the mitosis.

Or something.

"How in the stars have we been staying ahead of these things?" Khiry asked.

"You've assembled a great crew."

She shuddered, somewhat embarrassed by that reaction, somewhat embarrassed by thinking the tingles and tickles so recently on her spine had not been a response to Kor's nearness, but a response to the creature crawling on her.

"Gross," she said. How could she have mistaken something so ugly for reactions to Kor's advances?

"Are you okay?" he asked.

"It's just disgusting."

He still stood close to her and took advantage of the heroic save. Pulling her closer, he brushed his lips against her cheek and whispered, "You're safe, Khiry Okerson. I've got you."

This time, she knew the tingle that rushed up her spine belonged solely to her central nervous system.

CHAPTER FIVE

Even traveling at the Coronado's top speed, it took them the better part of two weeks to get to Annady.

Devin Alderman knew a spattering of the planet's recent history but hadn't visited it. Khiry surveyed the crew to learn no one else had been to Annady either, which was no surprise. She ended up on the bridge with Kor, Electra, and Mongoose, to discuss their options for checking out the new planet as they brought the ship close enough for orbit.

"Where do we want to land?" Mongoose asked. The security chief still filled in at one of the pilot chairs now that Frederick occupied the brig. She handled the additional position with confidence. Her practice and training on the cruise from Pangaea Moon to Earth had proved she was a fast learner.

"Not too far from the main colony," Khiry said. "Surely, they'll have built one main city with a number of surrounding cities after, what has it been? Twenty years? Twenty-five?"

Kor responded, "I don't know about that. The group on Eldora Prime just had the one city."

"Don't remind me," Electra muttered.

"Eldora Prime built a fortress around one capital city for protection," Khiry said. "Let's hope the help these terraformers have asked for isn't to fight off gross monsters from the mountains."

Little did she know how much she'd come to prefer fighting *gross monsters* to what Annady had in store for them.

"We're within range to scan," Electra said. "It looks like there's one concentration of humans on a mountainous continent. Lots of water. Lots. Similar to Earth, this planet is covered with water. Holy cow.

"Let's see...there's one, two, three main land masses...looks like a few smaller land groupings...island chains and such...but the biggest land mass has the big mountains to its north, an interior sea off to the northeast of the settlement, the concentration of humans, lots of arid land to their south. I've got, wait, yes, I've got a small group of humans with pangering life signs about a hundred miles north of the main group. Much smaller group of maybe ninety or a hundred life forms. But that's the only concentration of people on the whole planet. They stayed put, that's for sure."

"Then it sounds like that's the area we go to," Khiry decided. "Mongoose, set us down within eyesight of the main city."

"That'll be south of the city," Electra supplied. "Just a nudge to the right here."

"Got it," Mongoose said.

"Otherwise we'll be getting too close to that shelf there," Electra pointed at a ridge on the screen they both monitored.

"I see it. Looks steep, doesn't it?" Mongoose practically whispered, toggling the controls before her.

"They built pretty close to the ocean," Electra murmured to no one in particular.

"Setting up for exploration?" Mongoose asked her.

"Could be. If they saved enough materials from their transport ships for sailing."

"Lofty goals," Mongoose said. "Shutting the mix valve," she told the crew.

They watched the rounded form of Annady begin taking shape beneath a heavy gray cloud as they descended toward the planet.

"Are we sure the land is really land?" Khiry muttered. "It looks like one, complete, convex cloud."

"Cloud cover?" Kor suggested.

"Also…" Electra said. "Looks like great crop activity around the immediate east and north of them, lush greenery, but I'm getting a range of extra sulfate compounds in the atmosphere. I'm not sure what they're growing that's standing up to those kinds of gases in the air, but it looks like the soil is fantastic. Not the sand you'd expect near oceans."

Kor frowned at Khiry. "That sounds familiar. Why does sulfate sound familiar?"

Khiry shrugged. "It's not something prevalent in Earth's problems."

"No. And I don't think that's how I've heard of it," he said.

"It's the stuff from cows, isn't it?" Electra asked.

"Cows?" Mongoose asked.

"Naw. I think that's methane," Kor said. "And that's not how I've heard of it, either. I've heard that term 'sulfates' in relation to atmosphere before in old history books or something."

"If this ship had a reliable link to the bibliotecha, I'd look it up for you," Electra said.

"We can ask the good doctors when we next get a chance," Kor said. "They'll both give us a full lecture on it."

"No time for lectures," Mongoose announced. "We'll enter atmo in a minute."

As the Coronado moved through the clouded atmosphere, descending toward the planet, dark waters delineated chunky land masses. Like cracked black leather slowly breathing as one mass of skin, the ocean over which they passed barely rippled, barely moved, barely alluded to life.

As Mongoose deepened the angle of their descent, the blackness of the water turned a more brackish color, greener with burned algae far beneath its surface, and patches of dirty green earth took a crisper form.

"Now, do I set us down so Kor can watch us from the bridge or do I set us down so we can make a quick leap back on board if we need to?"

"Quick leap," Khiry supplied as Kor asked, "What makes you think I'm staying on the bridge?"

CHAPTER SIX

They landed at what equated to approaching dusk on their quadrant of Annady, yet they were met with pomp and circumstance as if the people of the colony had expected their timed arrival. These people didn't appear to be closing down the city for the night. The warm afternoon air still mixed with dust and the slight scent of too-old eggs as a city full of citizens paraded out to greet them.

Khiry stood at the top of the cargo bay ramp with Mongoose, Electra, Maubry, and the doctors, Devin and Max, in a small group. The dusty, sulfuric scent in the air tickled Khiry's nose, causing her to sneeze.

The planet had a heavy feel to its atmosphere, which she hadn't expected from a terraformable planet. Its gravity—or its air—pressed her bones down in her body. Even her ribcage pushed against her shirt, as if each bone had expanded with weight from this planet's heaviness.

The team had decided Electra and Khiry made the perfect partnership to greet the settlers. Devin and Max were the doctors who could offer the colonists medical attention if necessary. Mongoose offered security, of course.

Maubry could assist quickly with random technical issues in their city, as he currently fiddled with the lapel camera at his neck. A voice from the ship crackled from a tiny speaker alongside the camera: "You're transmitting now."

They hadn't expected what looked like the entire adult community to spill out of their neatly constructed wood and thatch homes and begin a march toward the ship.

"I feel like I'm in a musical," Devin offered, as the procession's grand marshal appeared.

Khiry wasn't sure what he meant, but she watched Dr. Max nod with enthusiasm. "Exactly," he agreed. "I expect dancing bears or something over-the-top like that to come out of nowhere."

Dancing bears? Khiry had heard stories of the way humans had once kept different types of animals as pets on Earth, but she couldn't imagine terraformers wasting time on such entertainment, once they got out among the stars. Surely they had more important things to focus on than training the non-humans around them for entertainment. Bears, horses, or even something as pet-oriented as dogs should be more useful performing tasks that helped with survival.

Terraformers needed working animals and working machines.

Of course, the late Captain Marlon of the Instigator had put dragons in a cage for some purpose—maybe for work, maybe for entertainment. Now Khiry carried three dragons around the universe in a spaceship. She glanced over her shoulder at the cargo bay door, where one of her reptilian crewmembers waited.

She and Kor had explained the best they could to Onyx and his large friend Nellie that the dragons were to stay hidden on board the ship until the humans knew what was going on at Annady. There was no point in endangering the creatures with the actions of frightened terraformers who might not have ever seen anything like a dragon before.

She looked over a community of about six thousand people who appeared genuinely happy to see the ship. They probably would have welcomed a handful of dragons coming out among the rest of the crew. The children of the community had a dance prepared, and they performed it ahead of the adults moving toward the Coronado in four sinuous columns.

There were no bears among them.

Even without bears, Khiry noticed a few odd things in the celebration marching toward them.

First, the eight-hundred or so children seemed to be in one age range; between what she figured was twelve and sixteen years of age, by her best guess. Of course, she had little confidence in her abilities to guess kids' ages.

Khiry would ask the doctors about it later, but she wondered if all the younger children were being held back, protected in their homes so the townspeople could make sure this new ship was truly on a mission of aid.

Second, the odd head dressings they wore reminded her of miniature collector arrays aboard the early cargo ships. Their skin-tight leotards of gray-silver polyester reminded her of old Yoga costumes. The youth looked like small receptors dancing around instead of receiving satellite information.

The abstract dance made her wonder what the head dressings were made of to appear so technical yet be light enough to rest upon the children's heads, while they undulated and skipped forward.

Third, the musical portion of the display came from drums and voices. That was all. No wooden, stringed instruments sounded, or horns trumpeted. Not even something as advanced as a gourd filled with pebbles graced the ceremony. And she saw plenty of stones and pebbles in the immediate vicinity for making such shakers. Considering the colony had begun with bright minds from Earth, she thought it strange that no one had brought musical instruments with them or had taken the time to create them, once on the new world.

"How long has Annady been terraformed?" she asked no one in particular.

Devin knew the specifics. "The first terraformers were shipped here twenty-three years ago with the basic staples. A second set of terraformers, including a few Panger System aliens, joined the original team two years later with additional staples. All that we see here is made from those basics and the planet's resources."

She nodded, wondering why it mattered to her that the citizens hadn't taken the time in twenty-three years to create more advanced musical instruments than drums. People who landed on a new world had to learn where to source minerals, how to predict weather patterns for food growth, which indigenous animals were likely to eat them, as well as which flora was poisonous and which benign.

They had to dismantle their original ships to build structures with the supplies they brought, and this group had to set up a reliable means of communication with Earth. There was little time for luxuries, unless passing ships brought them. Considering Annady's distance from any form of civilization—and The Debris Panel with its propensity for wrecking vessels—passing ships had not been a regular occurrence.

Despite the lack of time for niceties, the Annadians had obviously practiced the welcome routine they performed now. Berry-and-root-stained strips of cloth in varying shades of blue, magenta, and yellow adorned otherwise gray, skin-hugging garb of the adults, as the people danced in the glooming evening light toward the Coronado.

Khiry looked at Electra. "Do you get receptions like this a lot?"

Electra wore one of her diplomatic smiles. "More often than I like." She raised an arm to wave at the approaching lines of people. "But there's no way they can know I'm with this ship. They were expecting a different diplomat. Someone important must have been aboard the Eleos."

"They're gonna swarm the ship," Mongoose warned.

"They look organized," Maubry agreed.

"They look like they're ready for a party," Dr. Max said.

"Let's get out to them before they get to us," Khiry suggested. She lifted the back of her hand to her face as she led her group down the ramp and spoke into the comm on her wrist. "Adam, would you lift the ramp, please? Enough that no one's getting on board without our permission."

"Will do, Captain," her brother's voice responded from her wristplate. "Everything look okay?"

"Maybe," Khiry responded. "You guys can see this, right?"

"Barely," Kor's voice came back. "We have that odd angle."

"Adam should be able to bring us up on a camera. Keep an eye on what's going on."

"Will do, Captain."

She reminded the group around her, "Let's be careful what information we share."

"Understood," Devin murmured.

It took about half an hour to complete greetings with the leaders of the community because their joy overshadowed every word. Praises and gratitude rippled among the crowd. Their words of welcome included English and Hindi phrases from Earth.

Electra became the center of their celebration once she was introduced. It became apparent that the people believed El Presidente's sister had been sent specifically to their planet.

Khiry did nothing to change their belief. She allowed a set of the colony's leaders to take her team to a long, torchlit hall to continue the celebrating.

The hall consisted of two sections. The first could have been considered an Olympic sized porch, with open sides between thick, carved pillars holding up the wood and thatch roof. If the people hadn't spent time creating musical instruments, they had spent time adorning their central hall.

The second section, consuming only the back third of the structure, was the enclosed portion. It included an elaborate double door several feet taller than the typical human; and had a set of shuttered windows to either side of the grand doors. Even the wooden shutters were decorated and stained with color.

Above the door, someone had engraved the words "Laino Council of Annady" in precise and pretty English letters. Khiry could read enough Hindi to recognize the symbols beneath the English. They'd used the main languages of Earth, but not of the Panger System, to dedicate their central building in this mixed village.

She found that noteworthy.

None of the children were invited to this inner sanctuary. Khiry watched families breaking into excited groups, chattering and cheering as they dispersed. Many of the adults with offspring had more than one rambunctious youngling. In fact, the number of children in the teenage range made Khiry question what else the people of Annady had for entertainment, besides one another. While terraforming a planet would, of course, call for populating it with able-bodied and able-minded workers as quickly as possible, this seemed excessive.

She compared their clothing to her own. While the children seemed to be slightly younger than her, their clothing clung to their frames in an almost unsettling manner. But, to be fair, even the adults wore a manufactured cloth with vibrantly stained colors that hugged their bodies, as if massaging them as they moved.

Some of them had made fabric masks from the same stifling material to keep pollutants from entering their lungs, and the stretchy fabric outlined their noses, mouths, and chins in strange caricatures of human faces. Khiry noted how it differed from the loose, comfortable cotton shirt she wore. These people moved with a sometimes sensual and sometimes commanding purpose, as if advertising their prowess with the bright-colored stretches of material that outlined and defined their features and muscles.

While at least a hundred people crowded into the enclosed section of the hall, the woven rugs lining the floor, walls, chairs, and benches absorbed much of the noise, giving the impression of muffled chaos. The fabrics also absorbed the smoke from the high number of candles and torches supplying light. It lent a scent of smoky mustiness above the constant sulfur of this planet.

One member of the colony led Khiry and her crew to the rectangular table in the center of the room and introduced the group seated there as the Annady Council. At the head of the table sat an older man with thinned white hair and a form-fitting jacket over his high-collared shirt. Everything about him made it clear he was the leader of the Annady Council and colony, so the worker's introduction of him as Governor Arbaseys Laino surprised none of the Coronado crew.

A guard escorted Khiry to the middle of the crowded table where she sat with a dried gourd that had been made into a drum. At least, she assumed it was a drum.

She tapped her fingers against the thinnest section of it to elicit a gentle thrumming sound, similar to large raindrops against wood. It was pleasing, but difficult to hear above the voices celebrating the important emissary, Electra Endh.

She recorded in her memory the names of the council members as they were introduced: Mr. Tempel Pliny handled recording and reporting the colony's activities; Mr. Laurel Eidon handled security and discipline; Mrs. Sally Cobbler handled medical issues, yet was not the original doctor; Mrs. Cassidy Hopely's function was unclear to the crew at first; and Arbaseys Laino reigned over the rest.

"We rarely get news from Earth," someone was saying, "but we'd heard of your birthday celebration on Eldora Moon when we were seeking help. It made no sense then that the authorities on Earth would take time to share your movements during a communiqué about our disaster, but now that you're here, well, it all makes sense. What a momentous occasion! To have El Presidente's sister on a terraformed celestial body so much like ours. That was many months ago, and now you're here to help us!"

Khiry focused on the light drumming of her fingers against the skin to help drown out the extra voices and extra words and extra whoops of excitement — to bring just one voice at a time to her ears and to her brain. The people, who claimed to be elected officials for this society, were far too excited about the arrival of a group of teens with a pair of doctors. Among the many words of welcome, while watching a svelte young girl pour slick, slippery liquid into a torch's basin, she finally heard the reason.

"When your mother ship didn't appear last month," someone said clearly, "we feared no one would arrive before Vesuvius blows."

While Khiry didn't understand the reference to Vesuvius, she did recognize urgency and danger in what the person said. She signaled to Devin, who followed her a short distance away from the table. Thinking no one paid attention to them, she spoke lowly to the doctor, while everyone else continued celebrating.

"What do you know about someone named Vesuvius?" she asked her doctor.

"The Greek god from Earth mythology?" Devin asked.

She shrugged. "Did he cause dangerous windstorms? Or blow stuff up?"

"The volcano Vesuvius on Earth blew up in 79 A.D. It buried a lecherous and decadent society of Pompeii—"

She snapped her fingers. "That's what they meant."

Devin furrowed his brow. "Are you saying…"

She nodded. "These people think we're here to rescue them before a volcano erupts."

CHAPTER SEVEN

Before Annady's yellow-turned-ochre sunset gave way to darkness and black, Kor traded places with Dr. Max Sausen at Khiry's request. It had become obvious the terraformers weren't in dire need of doctors, and Khiry sensed an unrest that suggested extra muscle was a good idea.

Sunset on Annady was similar to that on Earth, even if it came at what equated to "early" for an earthling. At this time of year, the night would last at least fourteen hours, and the daylight approximately ten. The dwarf star around which Annady orbited had a yellow hue to it when viewed through the atmosphere of nitrogen, oxygen, argon, carbon dioxide, neon, methane, and helium. The group from the Coronado and a handful of older people from the community had settled into the hall at the outskirts of the city they'd landed near.

Time for celebrating was over.

They needed to figure out what to do for the Laino Colony.

Arbaseys Laino explained that he'd been the leader since the original transport ship had brought them to Annady twenty-three years before. While accepting a porcelain mug from the teen who had tended to the light in the room, the governor spoke to the child, looking in her eyes, but offering reassurance to the newcomers that the people on Annady were healthy. There was no plague or sickness that the doctors needed to treat.

Khiry wondered if the girl who pulled her hand away from the governor's was his granddaughter. She acted as if he'd chastised her recently, and now his forgiveness was unwelcome.

"Our only concern is escaping before catastrophe strikes," the apparent grandfather said, looking to Devin for acknowledgment.

"Governor, that has caught us by surprise," Khiry said.

Now, the aged man turned his attention from Devin, the oldest member of the Coronado crew, to a girl who appeared to speak out of turn.

"The catastrophe that's about to befall us?" Laino said.

The bushy, white line of hair over his eyes furrowed to show his exasperation. The expression caused the four lines of wrinkles that lay in messy rows parallel to his eyebrows to crinkle and crumple and dent downward toward his fleshy nose. His nostrils flared outward, and the flesh at the corners of his eyes rose in chunks of fatty deposits. He suddenly had the red-faced look of an elderly politician who screams to be heard when the substance of his message should be examined more closely.

No wonder a grandchild would have trouble accepting his calmer moments.

"I'm not sure how it could have surprised you, young lady. Didn't the captain tell you the details of the job?" He gestured toward Devin, as if expecting the man to take over the conversation.

Kor rose from the upholstered chair he'd assumed when joining the group and stood a few paces behind Khiry's seat. This gave him a good view of the table where Devin had been invited to sit with the governor and four other elders from the community. Khiry noticed Kor step out of her field of vision, and knew he moved to stand guard.

"Governor," she said. "There are a few things we need to clear up now that we have the privacy to talk."

"Do you have a plan for our evacuation?" a lady asked. She sat not far from the table and wore an expression of impatience. She wasn't as old as Laino but had obviously seen a few more decades than Khiry. Her shoulder-length blonde hair was streaked with gray and white strands that looked as if they'd break if someone tried to brush them into a fashionable style.

"Is that why you needed to meet with the elders in private?" Mrs. Cassidy Hopely continued. "To discuss the evacuation plan? I can assure you all the citizens in Laino Colony are ready to board the ships calmly and orderly. Captain," she looked directly at Devin, "you can send for the rest of the ships in all confidence that we are ready to go in a calm and orderly fashion. You'll not have any trouble or unruly behavior here, despite how late you've arrived."

The governor raised his hand to quiet her. "Cassidy, please. I'll speak for our people. But, truly, Captain Alderman, what she says is correct. We understand you must be concerned about the state our people are in, given how close Vesuvius is to critical, but we — the elders you see here — are in complete control of the colony. The people of Annady will be respectful of your evac plan. I'll make sure of it. Just give me the word and I'll put your plan into motion."

Devin offered his most diplomatic smile and held out his hand, gesturing to Khiry. "This is our captain. Khiry Okerson is the captain of the Coronado. I'm the doctor."

The five elders of Annady didn't try to hide their astonishment. The room filled with the sound of the torches guttering and Annady's nighttime bugs making their nighttime noises outside.

Mongoose knocked on the table in front of her. "Now that the shock of that is over, could we —"

"Wait a minute," Laino said. "Is this a joke? Are you testing us somehow? Is this a test?"

Khiry decided it was time to stop tossing ideas around in her brain and address the matter at hand. She sat up straight in her chair. "No, Governor, we're not testing you. I've let the officers from my crew visit with your people this past hour while I sorted out the best course of action at this point. I want to be perfectly frank with you. I want the five of you, as elders of the Annady community, to help me make the right plan for your people. The first thing I need to do is get more information. I think my questions will prove how little of that we have at this time.

"Let me start by asking about the volcano. I assume your scientists have been studying it closely. When do you think it's supposed to erupt?"

"Young lady," the governor said. "Are you saying you don't know how close we are to death?"

"I wouldn't phrase it that way, but that's what I'm trying to say."

The man shook his head in disbelief, calling attention to the reddening scalp under thin hair. "Our instruments show that mountain could blow any day. We've seen smoke plumes already. It's been spewing ash clouds for months, clouds that drift and cover everything. It's a wonder we can still breathe here."

"We have crates of boxes of surgical masks on our ship," Khiry said. "I'll see that they're made available to you immediately."

"We don't need face masks. We need to get away from the volcano. It will destroy this entire side of the continent when it takes apart the mountain range alongside our home and will send enough dross into the sky to make the rest of the planet uninhabitable for years."

"How can you know the volcano will have that kind of force?" she asked.

"As you pointed out, we have scientists among us," the governor snapped. "It's not difficult to predict the level of destruction coming upon us. Surely your sensors read the level of contaminants in the atmosphere already. Surely you noticed the lack of visibility and clarity in the air when you were landing. You must send for the rest of your armada and get us away from the blast…"

His voice trailed as Khiry averted her eyes.

"My God," he breathed. His voice lowered dramatically. "There are no other ships, are there? There is no armada."

No one moved. Khiry wasn't sure she wanted to answer that question. Even the child standing to the side of the room with the empty tray could see the six thousand people on the planet wouldn't fit on the Coronado. It would be better to let these people believe a fleet waited to rescue them.

Cassidy, who had spoken so calmly a few moments before, rose slowly from her place and walked to the lone window on the ocean side of the building, toward the Coronado. Sally followed and put a hand on her shoulder to comfort her. Cassidy stared out at the deepening nightfall with one hand covering her mouth, as if it prevented her from saying the words balanced on her tongue.

Khiry wondered for a second if the woman was one of those with children among the citizens of Annady. Did this lady have children out there that she now worried about saving from lava and fire?

"At this point, what I'd like to do is figure out how best to help you," Khiry said. "We came here in place of a ship called the Eleos, which…which ran into trouble leaving Earth."

"One ship?" Laino asked. "That makes no sense. When we sent for help, we explained that we needed a *full* evacuation. We were told to expect a *full* relocation."

"Who told you to expect this?" Khiry asked.

"The United Society for Peace and Strength. The missive came from authorities on Earth."

"And where were you to be taken?"

"Pangaea Moon," Laino hissed. As if catching himself in an act of treachery, he straightened his posture. "There are three colonized cities on Pangaea Moon with plenty more areas available for additional terraforming."

Electra put her hands together on the table in front of her. "Pangaea Moon is a long way from here."

"Everything is a long way from here," Laino said.

Khiry appreciated the fact he tempered his snarkiness when addressing Electra Endh.

"We were to stop at Earth so those who didn't wish to live in the Panger System could return to their lives in the Milky Way," Tempel said.

His suggestion was not lost on Khiry. Not everyone in the colony was pleased with the solution of relocating to the Panger System.

Devin frowned. "That's preposterous. Earth can't take anyone back at this point. They're still offloading as fast as they can."

Cassidy turned back to the table. "I don't understand. Why would the authorities offer us the opportunity to return to Earth to live among our own kind again, if such a life is no longer allowed? How can such a life not be allowed?"

Now, Maubry frowned. He didn't want to be an alarmist, but he recognized something unsettling in the way Cassidy's voice changed in pitch, alluding to her choice.

"The seas have continued to rise since you've been here on Annady," Khiry said. "The five-centimeter rise each year that scientists started documenting in the eighteen hundreds still wavers back and forth, like we've seen since 2020 on, as you all probably knew before you left the planet."

Her audience nodded, not interrupting.

"But the rise took a drastic turn recently. USPS scientists have discarded the U.S. Geological Survey's sea level predictions completely because they were on track until about 2050, when you all left for Annady, and then things went haywire. Sea level rise is increasing at a full quarter meter per year now. USGS predictions are moot in light of reality. What space Earth isn't using for living quarters, industry, or air purification is used for growing and raising food. The Earth you left twenty-three years ago has more crowded cities now than it did then."

"But haven't people been leaving to terraform other planets?" Cassidy insisted. "If people are still being sent off world, how can the cities still be overpopulated? We've received news reports from time to time that announce some new colony on some new place. Hasn't that been a constant directive?"

"To an extent," Devin said.

"That has been a constant source of problems," Electra said. "Since your ship brought you to Annady, corruption has entered the terraforming missions. My brother has fought that movement, with some success, but there are still members of the resistance who would work to see all terraforming stopped until different methods are perfected."

At the mention of Presidente Endh, the five colonists seemed to afford her more respect. As if they re-remembered who she was. Or maybe they reacted to her well-honed diplomatic skill. Khiry had appointed her the ship's communications liaison for all those reasons.

"There have been setbacks on Eldora Prime and Pangaea Moon recently," Electra continued. "The colony on Eldora Prime is a complete loss, in fact, but the settlements on Pangaea Moon have only to do minor repairs. That will be the logical place for your people to relocate, but I know a number of USPS ships are currently *en route* to the outposts in the far edges of the Panger System, which my brother tells me have suffered damages from solar storms.

"I don't tell you all of this to depress you, but to educate you on a situation you seem to have been kept ignorant of. The authorities should have kept you up to date. You should have been apprised of these developments. Perhaps your distance from Earth has made it difficult for communications, but that's not an excuse for USPS to ignore you or leave you out of the loop."

Laino had frowned through most of Electra's speech and found himself unable to stay silent. "I don't see how damaged space stations in the Panger System rate higher than an entire colony of earthlings about to be killed by a natural disaster."

Devin wasn't going to say it, but as a man of science who had studied world history, he had a frightening idea why the government would put technology repair ahead of people's lives.

Resources.

It pained him to think it, but the volcano on Annady was about to do the job of burying these pesky terraformers under several meters of pumice and lava. The government could write that off as a lesson learned about this planet and offload another six thousand people from Earth to somewhere else. He watched his captain come to the same conclusion, seeing the pale expression of distaste cross her face.

Khiry blinked her eyes slowly, before responding to the governor. "Did you express the severity of your situation to the authorities?"

"Of course, we did," the man snapped.

"And how long ago was that?" Khiry asked.

"At least three months ago."

"And when did they respond?"

"More than a full month afterward. It takes that long for communications from out here to go through the satellite relays around The Debris Panel. It's faster to get on a ship and jump into hyperdrive, but we haven't got a ship with hyperdrive capability."

Khiry nodded that she understood, still keeping a calm, steady demeanor. "And the response you received. It *was* a response from USPS?"

All five colonists signaled the affirmative. Despite their age and wisdom, the elders of Annady believed the government was going to save them.

Khiry needed more information: "In the response, they indicated they would send ships to evacuate you from this planet — taking you to Pangaea Moon via Earth?"

"Yes," Laino snapped. "We told you this. Yes. Anyone who wanted to go to Earth could stay on Earth."

"Governor, did you send a response *after* they indicated they were sending ships to evacuate you?"

The members of her crew didn't understand where their captain was going with this line of questioning, but all eyes were locked on Khiry at this point.

"Well…I believe we did. Cassidy, didn't we send a communiqué suggesting they hurry?"

The woman nodded. "Of course."

"And you would have sent that communication four weeks ago? Five?" Khiry asked.

Cassidy dropped to her chair then. "Are you suggesting they didn't get our last response?"

"I'm suggesting they may have only received your last response in the past two weeks…or they may not have received it at all. My point is, if they believed coming here to collect you was a lost cause, then sending the ships to the Panger System to repair technology would be their first priority. That's how the authorities think these days."

Maubry cleared his throat. "The authorities might also think you have a transport ship of your own here."

Laino snorted derisively. "The tiny transport vessel we brought in the original cargo hold was meant to move between close planets, or between a planet and its moon. And it's in a state of disrepair. It'll not get off the ground."

"Disrepair?" Maubry said. The engineer couldn't hide his incredulity.

"We have no use for the thing," Cassidy mumbled.

"You have a use for it now," Khiry offered, as gently as she could.

"The government should be sending an armada to save us," Laino hissed. "We have no need to waste time or precious materials on a decrepit piece of outdated technology that only a handful of our citizens could escape on."

Maubry and Khiry exchanged a silent communication before the engineer spoke again: "I'll take a look at your transport in the morning."

"If you like," Khiry quickly added. "Maubry can fix just about anything with an engine. Let's see if he can help out and double our carrying capacity that way."

Laino stared at Khiry. As if changing the subject to one that had just occurred to him, he said, "You are too young to be a spaceship captain. How did you get this mission in place of the Eleos? Is this a mission a little girl was sent on to fail?"

Ignoring the slew of insults built into the man's questions, Khiry shook her head. "We weren't given this job. We took up this mission without knowing what we would find here. That's why I have so many questions.

"We thought we were bringing whatever supplies we could offer to the terraformers here. I have two doctors aboard my ship; they could help if you had sickness. I've got a talented engineer. He could help you fix communications systems and spaceships. We never could have guessed that you wanted, that you needed, to evacuate a city full of people. And we certainly never would have guessed you wanted to take any of them back to Earth." She paused for a breath. "To stay."

CHAPTER EIGHT

Khiry and the off-ship team intended to return to the Coronado for the night, but the governor of Laino Colony insisted they accept his hospitality and stay with his people.

"We have room for you," Cassidy agreed with her leader.

Electra turned on her best diplomatic voice. "Governor Laino, Mrs. Hopely, we couldn't possibly impose on such short notice. We know you haven't the resources to entertain random crews from ships. The welcome we received when we landed was far more than we could have expected, and we're truly honored by it, but we can't expect anyone to make beds and further accommodations for us—"

"Nonsense," Cassidy interrupted her. "We have plenty of houses throughout the colony where you'll be comfortable for the night, and, as Governor Laino says, start fresh on our plans in the morning."

"Please don't wake anyone and ask them to open their home—" Electra began.

"Oh, no, you don't have to worry," Cassidy interrupted again. "We have homes that are empty. You could each have your own house for the night."

She spoke with a level of excitement that belied their situation.

A twinge of worry tweaked the base of Khiry's brain at the idea that the colony had houses available for them to show up and be made welcome at the drop of a hat. Khiry stayed silent, listening to the conversation unfold.

"We can get an early start," Tempel was saying.

"You can invite more of your crew to join us," Cassidy was saying.

"Our accommodations are quite cozy, despite what you may think of a terraforming colony this far from the Earth home base," Laino was saying.

None of their comments hinted at an ulterior motive. Khiry let Electra do the talking and turned to Mongoose. "Your thoughts?" she asked the security chief quietly.

Mongoose shook her head. "I think it's five by five. They want to keep track of us, that's certain, but just to settle their own nerves. We're their only hope."

Khiry nodded at that and signaled to Kor, who still stood on guard behind her.

He stepped forward and leaned in. "What are you thinking?" he asked.

"I'm thinking we need to let Coronado know we're staying the night."

"I'll handle that," he said.

"Thank you."

Khiry heard Electra make the final arrangement for the team to regroup shortly after dawn and turned her attention back to the table. They were rising to leave.

*　*　*　*　*

Although they were each offered a nice little house—with an indoor bathroom, Laino was quick to add—to stay in for the night, they wanted to stick together. They lived together on the ship; it felt strange to put solid walls and mud-brick streets between them.

Cassidy and Sally were the members of the Annady Council to understand their feelings on the matter. They agreed with Electra's proposal that the three ladies have a house together and the three men have one together.

"I think that's a smart idea," Cassidy said. "You're a team."

"What does a team have to do with anything?" Laino asked. "We have the accommodations to make them comfortable and to give them privacy they can't have access to aboard a transport ship—"

"Governor, splitting a team apart would be quite *un*comfortable," Cassidy supplied. She spoke cautiously, not out of any ulterior motive, as Khiry had already decided, but out of care not to offend the governor. It was clear she didn't want to go against his decision. Her suggestion was couched in calm, motherly tones. "By letting the ladies, especially, have a house together, you are demonstrating your keen understanding of their team bond. I applaud your willingness to work with them on this detail."

Khiry and Electra exchanged a quick nod. They had been colleagues for a span of three months, but they had faced death together in those three months. They knew in that quick exchange that they both saw the intelligence and manipulative skill of Mrs. Cassidy Hopely.

She was one of those wise women who only pretends to be subordinate to the bullying man in the room. Cassidy could call an audible when they needed her to.

Khiry also noticed the trio of guards posted outside the double doors of the building where they'd been meeting. When the group exited the walled portion of the hall, three men who appeared to be of the same age as the governor stood in a cluster with spears—actual spears made from trees and flint—as if to keep slow-moving predators at bay.

One of the guards, clean-shaven and muscular, reached out and shook the governor's hand. "Guv'nr," he said. "Nut'n mov'n out here."

Laino smiled tightly. "Excellent. Fine. Would you escort our guests to Alloy Street? They'll be staying in abandoned houses A and D."

"We'd be honored to," a second guard stated quickly. This lanky man thrust his hand out for Devin to shake. "I'm Justin Dreary," he continued, his tenor voice full of excitement. "At your service, Captain. If there's anything your team needs, I'll be at your service."

Before Devin could correct the man, Laino snapped at him. "Justin, you're embarrassing us all. This is their doctor." Apparently, the governor saw no need for Justin to be introduced to the captain, as he continued, "Get them to houses A and D and see that they're settled in comfortably for the night. And stand guard to be sure nothing disturbs their rest."

Justin took his correction in stride, merely nodding to the governor, which caused a chunk of black hair to drop into his eyes. He gestured for Devin—whether he was the leader or not—to step into the courtyard of guttering torches and recently swept stones. The citizens of Laino Colony had efficiently cleaned the detritus from the celebration while the council met with Khiry's crew, and now, no trace of raucous welcome could be seen.

Tidy, Khiry thought.

The group followed the three guards for a reasonable distance away from the ornate hall where Laino stayed with his sullen granddaughter and four depressed elders before Mongoose looked over her shoulder. "Don't think we're being followed," she said quietly to Khiry. "Shall I start asking questions?"

"Please. And start with what might show up to disturb our rest."

"On it," Mongoose confirmed. She skipped forward to come alongside the slender guard named Justin. Her short blonde hair sort of flopped against the bandana she wore tied in a simple knot at her neck. With her demeanor, one might mistake her for harmless.

"Howdy," she said. "I'm Misty. But everyone calls me Mongoose. You said you'd be at the captain's service if there was anything we needed?"

"Of course." The wideness of his vivid blue eyes proved she'd taken him by surprise. Whether that was due to her youth or her boldness, the group couldn't tell, but she would use it to her advantage at the moment.

"That's so great. You see, we've had to deal with pretty scary stuff on the last moon we set down on, and I'd like to make sure there's nothing gonna surprise us tonight. Are there animals or something you need those spears for?"

Direct, Khiry thought.

"Oh, these?" Justin wasn't recovered from his surprise yet.

Not a good sign, Khiry thought.

Kor nudged her with his elbow and spoke softly. "These guys strike you as hunters?"

She shook her head.

"Notice they've got supplies for us ready to go?"

"Yep," she replied just as quietly.

"Someone gave them the order to pack us a meal or two," Kor observed.

She nodded, watching the backpacks for any unnatural movement while they traveled through the colony. For some reason, she worried about the oversized spiders from her ship, as if those would be indigenous to Annady.

Justin fumbled his answer about the spears to Mongoose. "The guards carry these all the time. The spears are part of our uniform, if you will."

"I see," Mongoose answered him. "Why does Laino Colony need guards all the time?"

Khiry grinned.

Kor whispered, "Dang, she's good."

Justin was fumbling with his answer again, when the third guard, the one who'd been quiet until then, responded through a scruffy beard and mustache. "Any new planet has new dangers. As you said, when you set down on the last moon you visited, you encountered *scary stuff,* you called it? The same's true here.

"This planet has beasts the size of a small horse—you mighta called them ponies on Earth? Similar in size and shape to the ponies of Earth but covered in scales and able to spit fire, alternating with a venom that stings and paralyzes its victim for a number of hours." The man looked directly at Khiry. "Long enough for the victim to hold still while he's eaten. Alive."

Kor frowned, but Khiry didn't see him. She was looking at the scruffy guard trying to intimidate her.

Trying.

Failing.

"And these spears you carry can take down one of these ponies?" Khiry asked him, without breaking eye contact.

"Oh, we don't call them ponies. We call them scalers."

"I don't care what you call them," Khiry said. "I care what you use to stop them from killing your people."

"We haven't the luxury of laser guns and phase pistols out here on Annady, little lady. What juice we had for that kind of weaponry was used up long ago. Remember, we've been here over twenty years, most of us for twenty-three."

Mongoose didn't let him avoid Khiry's question any longer. She looked over her shoulder to ask, "If you're not using phase pistols, do the spears work for taking down these scalers?"

The guard sort of smiled, sort of grimaced at her from under his beard. "Sometimes."

Khiry heard Kor unsnap the leather strap that held his phase pistol in place on his belt. She had no such safety device to remove for her weapon; it was always at the ready.

Something about the conversation didn't set well with her. She didn't feel that they had gotten the answer to Mongoose's question. If spears worked sometimes, what else protected the people of the colony from pony-sized scalers?

"What's your name?" Khiry asked.

"I'm Branden." He nodded toward the guard who walked with Mongoose at the front of the party. "Justin introduced himself back at the hall. This here's Clint."

They continued walking the torch-lit streets past deep metal boxes of oils to keep torches glowing; past a low, slow fountain that barely bubbled; past a series of matching houses with dusty, shuttered windows; past a larger building that looked like a general store; past a garage where too many shadows held too many spare parts for the derelict transport vessel of two decades ago.

All the blueish shadows appeared dirtier and lumpier than they should thanks to a layer of powdery residue. It gave the colony a sense of abandonment, as if no humans stayed in this desolate place. Khiry expected a pony-sized beast to jump from one of the extra bays and fling venomous spittle at easy, unsuspecting prey.

No beasts jumped from anywhere, and they turned down a dusty street that had no bricks lining it for their feet. No torches glowed with welcoming light. No metal panels reflected the sparse starlight from above to explain the depth of shadows their bodies cast.

Six houses stood in eerie, uniform quiet on opposite sides of the path, as if nothing living had touched them for a dozen years. At the end of the short street, the dirt road gave way to bramble, rock, vegetation, and finally woods.

Mongoose and Kor instinctively took up their weapons and moved to either side of the party. The first house on the left side of the street had a giant letter A painted in red on the front door. The letter had faded to a splintered, rust-red color beneath dust and time.

"Reminds me of a story on the bibliotecha," Electra murmured.

On the opposite side of the dirt road, a second house boasted a giant letter D on its front door. These were to be their lodgings. Dark and quiet on a dark and quiet roadway, the abandoned structures had grown weary from holding up dust and secrets.

Khiry regretted the decision to stay the night in such a forlorn place. The sorrow radiating off these empty shells reached toward her and seeped into her skin. It made her joints ache to look at the open, sagging shutters that once would have blocked wind on a stormy day and welcomed sun and warmth on a pleasant day.

These houses told her all pleasant days were a thing of the past.

These houses asked her to move on to a better road—for safety's sake.

They stopped in front of the "A" house and Justin said, "I'll help the ladies get settled in here, if you want to take the gentlemen to—"

"Nope," Kor interrupted. "I'll go first."

CHAPTER NINE

"There's nothing to worry about," Justin assured Kor. "We've kept these houses in a state of readiness since sending the beacon for help, in case the rescue armada required some lodgings on the ground. They're clean and stocked with candles and toiletries —"

"It's not the level of cleanliness I'm worried about," Kor groused at the guard. As he noticed Khiry still walking alongside him toward the house, he glanced at her. "Will you stay here with the group?"

"Not on your life."

"Captain, please."

"I can order *you* to stay here," she suggested, still walking with him toward the wooden structure. Its brick-and-vegetation cobbled path leading from dirt road to door showed signs of cracking and breaking from ground that had heaved with seasons of neglect. They had to lift their feet carefully to avoid tripping on tufts of weeds between uneven bricks. Justin could try to convince them that the shelter itself was ready for guests, but the grounds were telling a different story in the sparse starlight.

As they approached, they noticed the sediment covering everything here stood thicker than what had coated the structures within the city proper. It resembled heavy, sooty sawdust, forming a layer on every surface from the simple brick step in front of the door to the frame around it, from one shutter dangling open on the front window to the pipe meant to collect water from the roof. A rain barrel sat with a thick layer of embers where the pipe fed into it, all carefully positioned and unmoved for years.

Justin stood to the side of the front door while Kor positioned Khiry behind him, a bit to the side, and slowly tilted the handle down. Of course, the door's hinges creaked as it opened. Why wouldn't they make an unholy sound to announce someone intruded here?

With the door open wide and the ominous sound fading to an echo, the three of them waited, listening, breathing, straining to hear any movement. The darkness of the house whispered nothing back. It greeted them with silence and a stronger scent of sulfur than what they'd breathed outside.

Kor grabbed a flashlight off his belt, clicked it on, and cut the black with the widening beam into the openness of the main, unfurnished room before them. Nothing moved. Nothing but silver dust floating in the beam's light.

"This house is one vacant room?" Kor asked quietly.

"The washroom and kitchen are behind that wall," Justin said, not bothering to moderate his voice. Khiry remembered Laino's pride concerning an indoor bathroom. She wondered if tacking an outhouse onto the back of a building made it "indoor," or if the terraformers had made efforts to perfect indoor plumbing when they hadn't bothered with electricity.

Justin stepped past the two of them. "Can you shine that to the right?"

Kor obliged, his beam revealing a closed door along the back wall.

Khiry heard nothing but the sound of Mongoose and Maubry's footsteps crunching along the brick path to join them. She grinned over her shoulder at Mongoose. *Didn't take long to override an order to wait,* Khiry thought. The security chief wasn't going to let her captain go into a strange, dark house without her.

Mongoose nodded once, and blonde hair dipped to her eyes. The powerhouse of muscle kept both hands on her weapon; she merely shook her head to toss her bangs to the side.

"Then to the left is the opening to the kitchen," Justin was saying. "They're all built the same way to make it easier."

Kor grunted his understanding as he stepped in behind the guard.

Khiry remembered a time her grandmother had complained about cookie-cutter houses. They'd been on one of the cargo-class transport ships running supplies to a rebel post on Eldora Moon. Grammie Okie had complained a lot. That evening she'd been on about how all the houses on Eldora were built to look the same so everyone would feel equally situated on the new colony. There was no diversity.

Khiry's mom had pulled her aside and told her not to listen to Grammie Okie. She'd said that the old woman had just been looking for things to argue about. The houses being all alike made them easier to put up and repair. It was easier to have replacement parts for hinges, toilets, light sockets, and the like, if each house had the same type of hinge, toilet, light socket, and the like.

Then they had arrived at the rebel area in a mountainous part of Eldora and nobody was even living in a house. Spare parts of broken ships propped up tents and lean-tos for the people who weren't living in holes under thick tree cover. Grammie Okie hadn't had much to say about diversity then.

Khiry shook off the memories of her family's differing opinions of USPS-sponsored housing on Eldora Moon and spoke to Mongoose. "Will you take a look around the perimeter? Let's secure just one unit to guard for the night."

"On it. Maubry, with me." She pointed at one of the guards, the non-scruffy one named Clint. "You. Go left. We're going right."

For some reason, the older man had no problem accepting the order from a seventeen-year-old female. Khiry made a mental note of that.

"Is there a door out the back?" Kor asked.

"Yes," Justin said. "Out the kitchen."

Kor glanced at Khiry. "We might be about to flush something out."

She nodded. "Mongoose."

"I hear ya. I won't shoot unless I know what it is."

With Mongoose, Maubry, and two guards circling the house, Kor, Khiry, and Justin continued their investigation inside. Devin stood at the front door with a knife as if he knew what to do with it, guarding Electra at his side. Justin went to the door at the back right of the front room—the door that led to the bathroom. Kor and Khiry moved to the door at the back left.

As the two men signaled to each other and pressed their respective doors open, Khiry realized a startling fact. They left no footprints on the wooden planks of the floor. The layer of cinders that settled on every surface outside didn't coat the floor inside.

She began to whisper, "I think someone's been clean—" when she was interrupted by a flurry of hoofbeats and shouts.

A blur of scaled motion burst from the kitchen.

Kor shouted his alarm as a mass of reptile knocked him to the floor. Four clawed feet thundered past him, barely missing his chest and head.

Justin raised his spear to throw it toward what looked like an enormous rock iguana erupting past Khiry, but a person thundered out of the bathroom, knocking Justin off balance and screaming a barbaric yawp.

The peace-shattering noise brought Mongoose and her team of scouts running from all sides. But just as quickly as noise and motion and chaos exploded in the main room, Khiry shouted above it all to quell it.

"Wait!" she yelled. "Wait!"

The horse-sized reptile galloping in place—facing Devin at the front door, turning to face Justin regaining his balance, spinning to see Devin again—let out a shriek of fear. The youth who had sprung out to protect the creature grabbed Justin's spear, screaming expletives and demanding he stop.

As Khiry suspected, the creature that had bounded past Kor, and then past her, had scales and wings and, lastly, a tail that had slapped her leg on its way by. This was a dragon. Smaller than Onyx or Nellie, but still a dragon.

"Wait!" she cried out again.

Mongoose and one of the guards had come in through the back, kitchen door. Mongoose didn't lower her weapon yet, but did reach down one hand to Kor.

Branden huffed and puffed through the front door behind Devin then, taking in a scene that had already come to a halt. He shouted, "Look out!" through his scraggly facial hair and let fly his spear. It carried with surprising force toward the largest being in the room.

It hit its mark.

The youth let go of the spear she fought Justin for and shrieked, as if she'd been hit instead.

CHAPTER TEN

On the bridge of the Coronado, Adam Okerson's head bowed toward the communications panel until his chin came within an inch of his chest.

Junior lifted his own chin to look up at the woman standing next to him, as if asking if they were going to wake the guy. She looked down at the reddish-brown juvenile dragon and grinned.

Chef Holly Phimmer had joined the crew while they were parked on Earth, but she understood the dynamic between Captain Okerson and her brother Adam pretty well already. The older brother had been a thorn in the captain's side at one point in life, had recently come around to be a decent human, and was now entrusted to watch over sensors and comms while the away team was on the planet outside.

That all made sense. But seeing Adam napping at his post was far too tempting an opportunity for mischief to pass up.

Holly winked at Junior and said, "Go get 'im."

With a gurgle of excitement, Junior bounced across the bridge and pounced onto the unsuspecting human. The uproar was spectacular.

Flailing arms, legs, and dragon tail threatened to take down the swivel chair Adam was falling out of. By the time the commotion settled, and Holly stopped laughing, Dr. Maxwell Sausen stood in the bridge doorway with a scowl.

"What's all this ruckus?"

Holly put a hand to his shoulder, still catching her breath.

"I didn't realize how much fun this job was gonna be."

"Fun is over," he said. He looked directly at Adam. "I just received a communication from Electra. Are you not monitoring their comms? Are their links not working? We need to get an injured dragon to our sick bay."

Adam and Holly sobered quickly.

*   *   *   *   *

In House A, it had taken more time to get everyone settled down. The youth who had jumped Justin, to protect the scaler taking up the space of two humans in their cabin, turned out to be a bona fide stowaway. It took Khiry and Electra several minutes to coax her name from her—Trilby—and to learn she was supposed to be at the second colony.

But that wasn't her only secret.

"I have to get this dragon back to the infirmary," Devin announced. "This wound is deep."

"No one can know!" Trilby screeched.

The dragon howled.

The three guards argued loudly with Kor and Mongoose. Maubry stepped close to Khiry to speak lowly, under the noise of arguing and angst. "I can take the moron who speared the dragon into custody."

"You're an engineer, not a sheriff," Khiry said. "Can you get Kor's attention?"

"I'll do you one better," Maubry said.

He faced the shadowy room where LED beams crisscrossed in haphazard cones of light and let out a piercing whistle. Everyone jumped or cringed or covered their ears as they spun their attention to the pangering. Because he stood next to Khiry, she now had the advantage of the floor.

"We need to calm down," she said. "This yelling will attract danger from the forest out there. *If* there's danger." She nodded toward the downed creature in their midst. "I'm getting the idea that maybe these scalers of yours interact with you more easily than you let on. Trilby, is this your pet?"

"No," the girl sniffled. "Goldie is my friend. You've killed my friend!" She shrieked at Branden in Kor's grip, and lunged for him, but Mongoose was as fast as her name suggested. She stepped between child and warrior, catching the girl in a hug.

"Okay, let's try to stay calm," Khiry said. She signaled to Kor that he could release his hold on Branden. "Trilby, we're getting help for Goldie. Electra?"

"Let me step outside to message the ship," Electra said. "It'll be quieter."

The team had worked together enough that Khiry didn't need to ask Devin and Maubry to begin tending to the wounded creature.

"Do your parents know you're out here by the abandoned houses with Goldie?" Khiry asked.

Trilby sniffled again, giving Khiry reason to worry about the girl's quick bounce between crazed, violent motion and subdued sadness. "No. My parents are at the other colony."

"The other? The one by the volcano?"

Trilby nodded. "I sneaked away. I came here when Dan brought minerals a while ago."

Khiry wasn't ready to ask who "Dan" was yet. "The other colony brings minerals to this one?"

Trilby nodded again, her eyes seeking the golden eyes of her dragon friend.

"Mongoose, let her…"

Mongoose understood, releasing the girl.

Trilby stepped to the moaning dragon's side and dropped to hug the creature's neck.

"How long have you been hiding out here with Goldie?"

Trilby sniffled an answer against the dragon's neck, but no one could understand her.

Mongoose stroked the girl's unkempt hair. "You poor dear. We're going to help your friend." She looked up at Khiry when the child made no response. "And we're going to help you, too. Do you need to get back to your parents?"

Trilby said, "I want to. I came here to find my friend." She glanced at Branden, as if afraid of him. "But I think she's dead."

"Has there been an accident?" Khiry asked, as gently as possible.

The clean-shaven guard cleared his throat. "Maybe we oughtta settle down for the night—"

Khiry cut him off. "Why does she think her friend is dead? What's going on here, Branden, Justin?"

"Nut'n's *going on*," Clint answered. "A runaway suppriz'd all us with'er pet scaler. Let's settle down and—"

Maubry interrupted him this time. "I don't know how it goes with earthlings, but it's never good to tell a pangering female to settle down."

Clint snarled at Khiry. "Yer a pang'ring?"

The click and whine of Kor's phase pistol pulled everyone's attention to the kitchen side of the house where Kor had leaned against the wall to watch the room. "If you know what's good for you, you'll be the one settling down."

Electra walked back in at that moment and took in the scene of Kor pointing a weapon at Clint. "Still tense in here. Ah, Captain, Dr. Max and Jevron will be here shortly. They're bringing a motorized cart to carry this one back to the ship. Are we all getting along in here?"

Khiry smirked. "Barely." She pointed at Clint. "It shouldn't matter what my lineage is; we're on this rock together. And at the moment, we're extremely calm. Now, I want to know why a young girl would run away from her family to find a friend in a colony a hundred miles away and then assume that friend was dead. What's going on in Laino Colony to make her think her friend has died here?"

CHAPTER ELEVEN

While Dr. Max, Devin, and Jevron bandaged the wound on Goldie the small dragon, preparing her for transport to the Coronado, Khiry distracted Trilby with her questions in the kitchen. The tiny room allowed a few people to sit on tall chairs on three sides of a plank-like table that folded down from the wall. Kor stood in the doorway, pointing a flashlight into the room at a metal, dome-shaped fixture suspended above the table.

Because of his angle from the close doorway, the light bounced off one half of the inner dome, but it served to offer decent illumination for the space. Wax build-up on the center of the table told them someone had used candles to perform the feat in the past.

At the table, Electra rummaged through one of the backpacks the guards had brought. She pulled out a leaf-wrapped item to investigate first. It looked like a sandwich.

"Can you tell me who you came to this colony to find?" Khiry asked as kindly as she could.

Trilby sniffled, wiping her nose with her sleeve. In the less-fractured light offered by Kor's flashlight-meets-dome epiphany, she could see that the girl's clothing was different from the snug, Spandex-like garments the members of Laino Colony wore.

Whatever fiber the colonists use to weave clothing must not be as plentiful up by the volcano, Khiry thought.

Trilby's clothing had a more flowing and billowier look to it. The fabric seemed to be made of softened or weathered fibers that didn't go through processing. When the girl dragged the sleeve across her face, the material absorbed her tears quickly.

"I'm not supposed to tell anyone who my friend is. It's a secret."

Electra offered her a napkin from the backpack, and said, "You know we're not from Laino Colony. Khiry and I won't get you or your friend into any trouble."

Khiry nodded. "We're here to help."

Trilby glanced at Kor, questioning his allegiance with her eyes.

"Kor is from our ship as well," Electra said. "The three of us have been together a while now."

Khiry thought it was clever of Electra not to go into detail there. While she felt a connection to Electra that belied a mere three months of friendship, that would be too difficult to explain to the girl while they were trying to extract information. It was easier to keep things vague.

"We came here to Annady to help however we could," Electra continued. "And we've found you all in danger from the volcano. We have no reason to tell on you or your friend for anything either of you is worried about. We can probably help you."

"I don't know about that," Trilby said softly. "We part-pangering kids are mixed kids. It's best that we stay out of sight and out of mind. That way, we don't offend anyone from the main colony." She lowered her voice to a whisper that the two ladies had to lean forward to hear. "No one's supposed to figure out how many of us mixed kids there are. No one's supposed to bring us to mind and cause trouble. No one's supposed to even know that Julia is who she is."

Electra frowned, but Khiry decided that was at least something to start with.

"Is she your sister?"

Trilby shook her head. "She's my friend's sister. Well, really, she's my friend, too. But no one's supposed to know that my friend has this sister. That's a secret that no one can know."

Khiry nodded. "I understand," she fibbed.

Thus far, she'd deduced the second, smaller colony must have more than different fabrics and clothes; the people there also had different children and different secrets. The youngster wiping her reddened nose and eyes with the napkin Electra had handed her showed stark fear of giving away those secrets. The messy, unwashed bangs that failed to hide her blood-shot eyes provided one more piece of evidence that this child hadn't been cared for, for many days.

"We won't tell anyone that the friend you seek is anyone's sister," Khiry reassured her. "She's a friend you're looking for."

Trilby visibly exhaled, her shoulders relaxing a measure.

"How old is your friend?" Electra asked.

"She's eight."

"That looks like she's younger than you, then?"

Trilby nodded. "Same as Jillian."

Khiry logged both names Trilby had given so far for future reference. Her confusion grew as the poor girl tried to keep secrets. "I noticed that a lot of the kids in Laino Colony are in the same age group. Are there a whole lot of kids at your colony?"

"Sort of. Just the ones that survive."

Khiry and Electra exchanged a worried look. Of course, it was known throughout the galaxies that mixers' babies didn't often survive birth. Trilby could be referencing that sad fact.

Or something more sinister could be behind her sadness.

"So, there are mixling children at your colony?" Khiry prompted. "And you try to hide?"

"Yes. I'm one. And that's why I can't tell anyone who my friend is." She glanced to the doorway, as if checking for eavesdropping guards. "She's a mixling, like her sister."

"Julia or Jillian?" Khiry asked.

Trilby physically reacted.

When she gasped and jumped at Khiry's use of the names, both Electra and Khiry jumped as well. The sudden fear was in complete contrast to the slow, quiet responses they'd been dragging out of the girl so far.

She practically shrieked, "How do you know their names?"

"It's okay," Electra said, placing a hand on Trilby's arm.

"You said their names just a second ago," Khiry explained. "It's okay. I won't say them again if you're worried. I just wanted to make sure…"

While Electra calmed Trilby again, Khiry stepped the short distance to Kor. "Is Maubry still, ah, I see him. Maubry?"

The engineer strode from the guards he'd been questioning to his captain. "What do you need? Something else happen?"

"I'm not sure what all's going on around here, but I'm more uneasy about this Laino Colony now that I've talked to Trilby for a bit. I want to get a team up to the second colony somehow. We probably need to come up with an excuse to make that happen, but when we do, I need you to get the mix out of the engines, so no one steals our ship out from under us."

Maubry nodded while she spoke. "All that makes all kinds of sense."

"I agree," Kor said. "Do you think we need to have Jevron get the engines cleared tonight?"

"They've got Goldie on the stretcher," Maubry offered. "I could jog out there and ask him to take care of that when they get her to the ship."

"I like that," Khiry said. "And I think Trilby's gonna want to go with her dragon."

She wasn't wrong. The young girl walked to the Coronado alongside her injured dragon friend with the two doctors and Jevron. The rest of the Coronado officers managed to settle their nerves enough for light sleep and turns standing guard with the three Annadians.

By the time the sun peered over the landscape to drench them in morning light, they each felt more tired, more uncomfortable, and more concerned about their mission than the night before. Something in nature tickled the hairs on the back of Khiry's neck as she took her turn in the much-acclaimed indoor bathroom. As she stepped back into the main room of House A, she learned why. Kor strode in from the front door with a scowl.

"That mountain's doing something," he warned.

The ground didn't shake hard enough to knock her off her feet, but the unmistakable trembling of a volcano stretching its muscles put her on guard.

"There's more smoke," Justin shouted from the front step.

He did not sound calm.

CHAPTER TWELVE

"In the bright light of day, their situation looks even worse," Kor told her.

"Their situation and the cloud rising from the mountains," Khiry agreed.

Her gesture toward the north drew his gaze up from the bustling colonists and toward the late morning sun. A gray haze didn't quite blot out the sun, but it shadowed all the ground and air around them, as if they sat on the edge of an eclipse's path of annularity. Khiry imagined she sat beneath an ever-present gauze umbrella—one that slowly descended with a sickening promise to suffocate her beneath dust and despair.

She sat on a convenient dent in, and leaned against, a boulder on the outskirts of the main colony, watching a number of Annadians going about the duties of gathering and packing. The communication device on her ear crackled.

"It's unfair to let them think they're saved," she continued, bending her arm to tap the device.

Kor stood next to her, leaning easily against the boulder with his arms crossed in a lazy, almost comfortable position. Looking at them from the colony several hundred meters away, one might mistake them for being off-guard or at-ease. He spoke quietly, "If they knew the whole truth, these people would swarm our ship and kill us to save themselves."

"I have more faith in humanity than that," she said, wincing from the crackling that sounded like maracas shaking against her eardrum.

"Faith in humanity?" he asked. "Or innocence?"

"What?"

Without taking his eyes from the groups moving between buildings to their north, Kor asked: "Are you so innocent that you think these people won't kill us to save themselves?"

Khiry thought about that for a minute. "I like the idea that you consider me innocent—not capable of the violence you accuse them of."

"I see their governor headed this way. You might need to practice a bit of violence."

"Devin wouldn't forgive me."

"Forgive you for what?" Devin's voice asked from her right shoulder.

Despite her heightened senses, the suddenness of the doctor's appearance startled her. "For pity's sake, Devin."

"Sorry, Captain. You can't hear my footsteps out here on dirt the way you can on the ship."

"Apparently not."

"Or she's tense," Kor suggested.

"Khiry, can you hear me?" Electra's voice spoke through her earpiece, minus the crackling this time.

"Ah, now I can hear you," Khiry said, holding the device steady against her ear. "The comm was breaking up."

"The activity we're reading from the volcano is settling down again," Electra reported. "This morning's plume should be all we see for a while."

"For a while?" Khiry asked. "What do we define as a while?"

"Four days?" Electra's voice suggested in her ear. "That's what Dr. Max guesses from the low—oh, wait—I'm to say, that's what Dr. Max can estimate from the current readings."

Khiry couldn't help grinning at the exchange she figured took place on the bridge. "Understood. Thank you."

Electra continued: "I sent Devin out there to speak to you because I couldn't get this comm to work. Even though the volcano doesn't look like it's going full-out for four days, the second colony just south of it is definitely silent. No radio contact, no movement."

"Understood." Khiry lowered her hand to a position closer to her weapon while they watched the governor approaching, but she told Kor and Devin, "Electra says that little burp from Vesuvius this morning is all we should see for a while."

"Is that 'little burp' what's messing with the comms; what's wrong with all our devices?" Kor asked.

Devin shook his head. "I'd hazard a guess our problem is those blasted spiders."

Khiry's jaw tightened. "I thought they were dead."

"We've been finding pockets of them in the craziest places. When we got Goldie and Trilby to the ship last night, we saw a mass of them all webbed up in this stringy, webby, mounded—"

"Okay, okay, I don't need that visual," Khiry stopped him. "We really need the ship for escaping this planet, so we've got to do something about the spider problem. Would you ask Jevron to lead a team for that? Let's make it a goal to clear out every last one of those spiders before we lift off."

"I'll give him your order," Devin said.

"Captain Okerson," Laino called as he neared them. "I have an idea for you."

Khiry was almost thankful to put ugly arachnids out of her mind. "Thank goodness. My ideas are coming up empty so far."

The smugness in the older man's smile won him no friends among the trio, but they weren't listening to become pals. They were listening to help save people.

"I know you can't get all of my people aboard this one small ship, but we keep an updated census of the citizens in the Laino Colony. I have Cassidy going through the census right now, picking out the most important people to the survival of—"

"Whoa," Kor interrupted him.

"I'm sure I don't want to hear the rest of that," Khiry said.

"Of course. Of course. These matters are distressing to us all. I don't like the concept of selecting who will live and who will die any more than you do," the governor lied with a smooth curve to his lips. "But the fact remains you can't get all of these people aboard this one cargo ship. So, whom do we save? Whom do we take aboard? The entire populace has been waiting for an armada's arrival. How do we announce to them you failed to bring an armada and only a portion of them can be saved?"

Devin put his hands to his face and massaged his cheeks and temple. The motion wasn't lost to Khiry. She saw that the doctor struggled with the idea.

"I appreciate that you're torn over how to save as many of your people as you can," she said. She wanted to give the governor the benefit of the doubt. She wanted to believe he tried to save others, not merely himself. "I don't see how we can select from your population when nearly a hundred of your citizens aren't even in the city."

Laino narrowed his eyes, hesitating before asking, "What do you mean?"

"The people to the north of here. We noticed a group about a hundred miles north of this main colony as we neared the planet. We discussed their predicament with your guards last night, but they seemed unable to talk about the peoples' mobility, their transportability, even how to get a message to them in any sort of efficient manner. How quickly can we expect them to get back to the city? Do they have reliable motorized transportation other than what they bring minerals with?"

The governor considered this a moment, glancing to the dirt at the right of Khiry's feet, before looking back at her face. "There's no guarantee they'll be able to get back before Vesuvius blows."

"Especially if they don't realize the magnitude of what's wrong," Khiry said. She pretended not to notice the surprised look Kor shot her way. "Electra Endh let me know that the community to our north hasn't moved, hasn't radioed for help. Do you know why they would stay where they're in danger, rather than return to the main colony here?"

"We don't have much contact with that group," Laino said.

"Are they up there in the mountains to study the volcano?"

All three of the Coronado's crew felt him hesitate ever-so-slightly before saying, "Yes, but that doesn't mean they're staying close to danger on purpose."

"On purpose?" she asked.

"I don't know what they're doing," Laino snapped. "But we must certainly send them a message that you've arrived, if you think we should bother."

"If I think we should bother? Have you tried to reach them yet to tell them we're here? They're your people. You can't leave them behind any more than you can leave your neighbor—"

"Of course," he interrupted. "You're right. I see your point."

Khiry glanced at Kor, who appeared ready to use the boulder as a launch pad to tackle the governor making such patronizing statements.

"Let me have Laurel signal their outpost when I get back to my town hall. I'll think of what we can say to them. I'd like to tell them we're planning on pulling names from a hat, then? Is that what you'd suggest, instead of the census Cassidy's been laboring on since last night?"

"I can't imagine pulling names out of a hat will be any kinder, but it's fairer," Kor said.

"It's like a lottery then," Laino said. "We put the first thousand people on your ship and go to the nearest port. Drop us off, refuel, return for more people. The next thousand climb aboard."

"That plan makes sense on the surface of it," Khiry said. "But you must know the five thousand people you leave behind will go insane with fear. And the nearest port is too far away for us to support a thousand people."

"Then we take five hundred," Laino argued. "And you're discounting the idea that you'll meet up with the Eleos on its way here."

"The Eleos isn't coming," Kor said.

"You can't know that."

"We do know that," Khiry said. "The Eleos was destroyed."

The governor hung his head for a moment, which gave Khiry time to think maybe he prayed for the souls lost aboard the ship. Then he looked back up at them. "I haven't the luxury of time to dwell on the implications of that."

Not praying for others, Khiry thought.

"But there are other ships in the universe," the governor continued. "One of them might run across us while we're out there."

Khiry sighed. "The law of averages would say otherwise. We have limited time to come up with a viable option—"

"Law of averages? You!" Laino sputtered. It was obvious he'd lost his diplomatic air. "Some teenage girl who shipped around the stars with thieves and taggers, and never went to a real school, is going to tell me something about the law of averages? Can you even quote what it is?"

Devin put a hand out to stop anyone else from speaking. "Here now. Whether someone can quote a law verbatim or not means nothing. The captain understands the concept and she's trying to explain to you something that she knows better than any one of us standing here. No ship is flying around out there in this sector looking for some humanitarian mission to take on. You're lucky we're here. You're lucky we landed. You're lucky we're entertaining your ideas. We want to help you however we can. Now let's put together some constructive ideas to save as many people as we can."

The governor didn't look happy to Khiry. She knew she had to come up with some way to settle the issue or things were going to come down to weapons fire and the blood of innocent people on her crewmembers' hands. She didn't want to put any more pressure on her crew. It wasn't fair to ask any more horrible things of them.

"Here's what I can do," Laino said, as if solving the problem on his own. "I'll see what Cassidy has come up with on the census so far. I'll clear it of any mixlings and prepare the computer to randomly draw five hundred citizens' names from the list. We don't typically waste electricity using outdated technology like that, but you don't give me much choice, do you? I'll have the five-hundred ready to go by dawn. To be honest, I think most of us are ready to go right now. There won't be much to do for preparations at this point."

Khiry nodded, but wanted to buy more time. Even five hundred citizens would tax the Coronado's supplies and life support systems, plus fuel. They'd never make it to a port with that number of extra bodies on board.

She needed a different plan. And what was this comment about mixlings? Was he acknowledging mixlings were alive in this community? That this colony had birthed mixlings who survived?

"Um…It would be novel to meet a mixling," Khiry said.

"Of course, it would be. On Earth they die. Here we typically don't know they're happening until it's too late. We have a spattering of them in the community that have survived."

"You sound disappointed by that," Devin said.

Laino shrugged and delivered a practiced speech: "I'm not so much disappointed as I am resigned to the fact that members of my community have set themselves up for heartbreak when their children eventually succumb to internal defects. I can't govern who they choose to build a family with, no matter how short-lived that family may be. And now, it appears it's not going to matter when Vesuvius erupts."

"May my doctor meet one from your colony?" Khiry asked.

The narrowed gaze he studied her with gave Khiry pause. Had she overplayed her hand? Did one of the guards—probably Clint—tell the governor that the child they'd found at the outskirts of the city was likely a mixling—and now occupied the Coronado's infirmary with a scaler beast?

"A mixling?" he asked. "Why?"

"Technology," Khiry answered quickly.

Laino nodded. "I'll see to it."

They watched him journey back toward the main city, and Khiry waited until he was out of hearing to ask, "Why don't these people use vehicles?"

"No fuel?" Kor suggested.

"Maybe. But there's plenty of solar power to capture. That man right there strikes me as the type who motors around in a solar-powered vehicle all the time while the underlings walk on the dirty paths of the city." They all watched him getting smaller as he moved further away. "He doesn't like to let his feet get dirty."

"Until now? He seems okay with walking around instead of shuttling around in a hovercraft," Devin said.

"Maybe," she said again. "I think he's acting a part."

"The part of a jerk," Kor said.

"Be that as it may," Devin said. "He's on his way to rig a computer to pull five hundred names of his favorite citizens for us to put on our ship in the morning. Are we okay with that?"

"Of course not," Kor and Khiry said in unison.

"So, what will we do in the morning when he marches up to the ship with five hundred people and their luggage?"

Khiry frowned at her doctor. "We'll have a plan by then."

CHAPTER THIRTEEN

Maubry and Mongoose updated Khiry on their plan to work with the guard named Branden and another Annadian to bring the derelict transport vessel back to working order. Khiry stood at the base of the cargo bay ramp, vividly aware that Onyx paced in his lumbering dragon waddle at the top of the ramp, waiting for her.

"I got the impression they've got plenty of scrap materials," Khiry said. "Nuts and bolts kind of scraps and such. But anything they need to get their ship flight-ready, use it. If we have it, take it over there and use it."

"Understood, Captain," Maubry said.

Khiry put a hand on Mongoose's shoulder. "You realize it's vital to watch his six while he's working?"

Mongoose offered a grin of mischief-mixed-with-understanding. "I won't let them kidnap our chief engineer."

Kor had squeezed past Onyx and made it half-way down the ramp during this exchange. "Ah, discussing how much trust we've placed in our neighbors?" He handed a metal box to Mongoose, saying, "Food from Holly," in explanation of it.

"There'll be at least two of them watching him repair their little ship," Khiry said. "If they see how good he is at it, they'll want to keep him."

Maubry couldn't help standing a little taller while they talked about him, right in front of him. He also couldn't help blushing under the praise. "Well, let's get a move-on, then."

Mongoose winked at her captain as the two lifted heavy duffel bags of clanking tools and parts to their backs and began walking north to the colony.

"Electra tells me you're going to the health center for some reason?" Kor said.

"Yeah, I want to check on some records. That comment Laino made about making sure no mixlings were on their lottery list didn't set well with me. He must know of more than the three he mentioned…"

Kor watched her think on this for a moment. Watched her until Onyx hooted his impatient displeasure from behind them.

*   *   *   *   *

While Khiry visited the health center in the colony, with Onyx as her towering bodyguard, Dr. Devin Alderman and Dr. Max Sausen cleared the small dragon named Goldie for travel. Of course, they all needed to figure out to where the dragon would travel, but the first order of business was to close a wound incurred during the night.

In the infirmary with its bright overhead lighting, the two doctors sat on either side of Goldie's chunky, reptile body. Trilby's demeanor had changed considerably from the night before.

Her smile filled her whole face. In one hand, she held a doll made of a hand towel and cleverly tied strings of jute; in the other, she held an apple tart. Both were gifts from the chef, who had asked what food Goldie would like before going back to the infirmary to see what could be created.

"I can't believe you have a chef who will make food for your dragons," Trilby said.

From behind Dr. Max, Lacy and Junior watched. Despite his young age—and propensity to good off—Junior had been invited to keep Goldie at ease during the "harsher" part of the operation this morning. Lacy was there to calm Trilby.

"She came on board when we were on Earth," Lacy said. "And the first thing she asked me was what my favorite kind of cake is. I love cake."

Trilby offered half of her apple tart to Goldie, who wasted no time slurping it from the girl's hand with her tongue. "How many flavors of cake are there to choose from?"

Lacy's gasp made Dr. Max snicker.

"You don't know about cake?"

"I've had birthday cake that Doctor Crystal made for us kids."

"Cake makes everything better," Lacy said with more wisdom than her years would have suggested. "When we got away from Pangaea Moon, when we knew my mom and dad were dead from the plague and that I was gonna be alone now, Captain Khiry helped me bake a cake in the galley. We took a lot of time to make food for the other people who are still alive while we flew to Earth."

Lacy leaned against Junior while she spoke, and the young dragon had no problem holding her weight. "She told me I'm part of the Coronado crew now unless I want to live with my grandparents, if we can find them, and I can be part of this family so I'm not all alone. She's also the one who told me cake makes everything better. She's right about a lot of stuff. If your parents don't make it to the ship, you won't be alone here."

Dr. Max cleared his throat to interrupt the somewhat-depressing soliloquy. "I'm sure the team is doing their best to find Trilby's parents. And I think we're just about done mending this fine dragon."

Devin patted Goldie's neck at this point and said, "My friend, your wound will heal nicely. The local sedative should start to wear off and you'll feel the pull of these stitches. They're not what I'd prefer, but…"

"But you have formidable skin that requires great energy to heal," Dr. Max finished. "We had to use strong ties to bind your wound."

Devin raised an eyebrow to question his friend, who shrugged back.

Trilby sat up a little taller on the table in front of Goldie. She liked the words Dr. Max used.

"You sound like our captain," Devin suggested.

Dr. Max grinned. "That's where I learned how to talk to dragons."

CHAPTER FOURTEEN

The following morning proved Khiry had been right about developing a plan. She wanted one that moved the mixling children out of harm's way and set the Annadians at ease. The last thing she needed was to have six thousand frightened people swarm the ship, as Kor suggested they might.

Khiry had tossed and turned through a sleepless night on board her ship, listening for sounds of potential stowaways between random thwacks of her crewmembers killing spiders.

The cleansing scent of essential oil of rosemary still hung faintly enough in the air vents to mask the planet's sulfur smell trying to seep on board, but she imagined and dreamt of stinky humidity droplets rolling like condensation down the bulbous windows of the bridge. Her frazzled nerves convinced her the snores of Onyx on the bridge outside her cabin drowned out too many important sounds; she had to rise and start the day that would take her to the second colony.

A fast shower in the Coronado's washroom cleansed her of Annady's dust but didn't take all the grit out of her hair. A sense of harshness clung to her even as she put on clean pants and a fresh, loose, cream-colored blouse.

With a spin of her wrist, she tucked her knife into its sheath at her belt to complete her look of a space cowgirl, rather than a ship captain, and hurried to a group of Annadians near the cargo bay ramp. Maubry and Mongoose stood on opposite sides of a solar-powered jeep just beyond the metal plank, paused in their early morning loading of goods onto the mini-tractor trailing the vehicle.

"We have a ton of tools and parts in our cargo hold because we *were* taking them to Pangaea Moon for repairs," Maubry was arguing. "If we can use those supplies to modify and beef up their transports, we can get people back here double-time. Like the captain said…" He nodded in her direction to acknowledge her arrival. "That makes room in our ship for more people and gets more of your people away from the volcano."

"And like I have said, there's no time for such shenanigans," Laino spat. "You can move whatever useless detritus you brought to this field and start loading people from this colony as soon as we complete the lottery. No time wasted."

"The sensors say we've got time to save—"

"Young man, I've been on this planet longer than you've been alive. I can tell you that I know its idiosyncrasies."

Maubry put both fists on his hips, which made his tattooed biceps bulge. Whether he intended to look like an intimidating pangering or not, the effect put the Annady elders in attendance on notice.

"I don't doubt that," Maubry said. "What I'm saying is our ship has the ability to read the actual tectonic plates under the ground. The sensors aboard the Coronado are telling us we have at least seventy-two hours before any pressure buildup will reach a level close enough to move anything. We have at least seventy-two hours before anything's gonna move. And then the movement—"

"Your cargo ship's sensors cannot predict the impact a planet's core buildup will have on the surface," Laino shouted from a reddened face.

Mongoose leaned close to Khiry's ear. "Just like we humans cannot predict the impact a governor's bruised ego will have on a coup to overtake our ship."

Khiry took the hint. She spoke softly back to Mongoose, "Do you know if Jevron got the mix out of the engines so no one's lifting off this planet without a great deal of effort or know-how?"

Mongoose nodded. "It's done."

To the rest of the group, Khiry spoke up in a voice not to be missed: "Gentlemen, please. I have utmost confidence in the combined efficiency of Electra Endh, the historian Tempel Pliny, and the Coronado's sensor readings to alert us if anything should change in Annady's core, lithosphere, or anywhere. The sooner we get moving, the sooner we can get off world. Governor Laino, can I count on you to ready the team rebuilding your transport ship here? And Mrs. Hopely, can I count on you to prepare the first and second set of citizens for travel?"

Laino offered one of his tight, patronizing smiles. Cassidy answered, "Of course. That process is already underway. I'm happy to—"

"We know how to run our colony," Laino cut in.

"While my away team is checking on the secondary colony, could I ask a favor of you?" Khiry asked. She motioned for Laino to step aside with her, which, to her surprise, he did.

"What additional favors do you require while we prepare for survival?"

Ignoring his hint at martyrdom, she said, "I understand you have *three* mixling children in the colony."

She expected his stiffened response. The taller stance, deep intake of breath, tightened lips, flared nostrils.

"I'm sure you don't share this prejudice," she lied, "but there are some in your colony who have made it clear that they don't like the mixing of human and pangering bloodlines. I think we could ease some of their 'discomfort' if we gave the impression that the three are being set aside."

"Go on."

"I mentioned yesterday my interest in meeting one of these children, but I have an ulterior motive here. You are aware that any doctor who can offer scientific information, real facts, about surviving mixlings could get any request he wants granted from the USPS?"

Laino stared hard at her face, which sent the hairs on the back of her neck to attention.

"I suggest we let Devin and Dr. Max study the three mixlings aboard the Coronado," she said. "Let them get some data. Let them fire information around The Debris Panel back to Earth. The information might get there before us, it might not. It might buy us help before Vesuvius blows, it might not. But it's a nice backup plan."

He nodded tersely. "I'll have the three sent to your ship at once."

As he turned on his heel to leave her, Khiry felt the need to brush her teeth. And not from the residue coating every surface around her. She wanted to wash the dirty deception out of her mouth.

Instead, she watched her crew working toward the plan to help as many people as they could. She saw her brother Adam and a crewman named Leo carrying toolboxes and grease guns toward the city.

They would spend a second day working on the colony's old transport as Maubry had instructed them. She knew they could repair a small transport, but she didn't know if they could do it in less than seventy-two hours. Then, the team was going to need a significant fuel source to get a second ship off the ground.

She couldn't hear the conversations going on around the jeep or the Coronado at this point, but she could see the team still prepared to journey north. She went to find Onyx aboard the ship; the dragon would make an excellent companion on the hundred-mile trip toward the secondary colony.

Devin and Dr. Max walked toward the solar jeep, each carrying a box — one marked "surgical masks" and one marked "slides."

"That's the last of the supplies, then?" Maubry asked.

"Think so," Dr. Max answered. "It's hard to get a straight answer on what those folks'll need."

"That's a fact," Maubry said. "And if that governor fellow tells Khiry this is a waste of time once more, she's gonna spang him."

Dr. Max grumbled while he shifted boxes and crates around in the back of the jeep, adjusting medical supplies and tools around the solar cell. "That governor fellow needs to be jailed until we're ready to leave."

"We should've thought our plan through a little better," Devin said. "That group up north probably needs both of us."

Dr. Max shook his head. "Probably. But Trilby mentioned a Dr. Crystal at the other colony I can connect with. And there's no point putting both of us in danger up there. You stay here to carry out the farce with the kids. I'll see what I can do for the people at the secondary colony." He smiled and clapped his friend on the shoulder. "It'll be all right. Even with a shorter daylight window on this planet, seventy-two hours is plenty of time."

CHAPTER FIFTEEN

Khiry sat shotgun. To make it convincing, she held her plasma pistol on her lap. With Justin driving, she could keep an eye on his hands and the path that passed for a road through the subtly marked terrain.

Skinny cypress trees no bigger round than one of Khiry's legs leaned haphazardly over the sandy path, as if they once guarded the forest but had lately surrendered to suffocation and apathy. Their skinnier branches wept twigs and pine needles in the process of falling off in alopecic chunks to litter the path with something for the jeep's tires to grip.

The skeletal trees gave the thicker parts of the forest to the left and right of the path a ghostly aura. As if the Panger mercies watched sadly, waiting for souls to carry home.

In the open back half of the jeep, Kor and Maubry sat on either side of the solar fixture. Both were armed and alert and wedged between boxes of medical and food supplies. Every once in a while, Kor shooed an insect off the solar cell's plexiglass covering or wiped away a light coating of ash.

Maubry finally grinned at him. "You know that doesn't really matter, right?"

Mongoose and Dr. Max sat amid more boxes and bags on the trailer they towed, both armed and alert and obviously holding on for dear life. The trailer didn't have the same center of gravity the jeep did.

Onyx, circling above, could have added the weight needed to keep the trailer from jolting and jostling them into nausea, but he also would have added the weight that would slow them from their fifty-mile-an-hour pace to something closer to a crawl. At least, it would slow them to a crawl more often.

Khiry grew agitated by the frequency with which they had to slow their pace to get through downed, dying brush or climb mounds of sand that had blown over the path.

"I think it's been several years since anyone's been up to see these people," she finally announced, above the noise of spinning tires and engine's whir.

Justin grimaced, straining to control the steering wheel as they lurched over a low dune. "I can't remember the purpose of the last visit to them. They bring minerals to us on the reg, so this path should be better maintained."

"They're in charge of road maintenance?" she asked.

"Yes, in fact, they are. The secondary colony is to maintain the corridor to and from Laino Colony. This is unacceptable."

"This is ash," Dr. Max yelled to the front. His voice shook as the trailer roughed him up.

Onyx landed a quarter of a mile ahead of the jeep, effectively blocking their path and growling a warning.

"I think we're on the wrong road," Khiry muttered. "Follow my dragon, Justin."

"This is the only corridor through the forest."

"Onyx is telling us otherwise."

"I'm telling you. I've done this trip before. It was a while back, but I drove the jeep up here along this road through this forest. It's rough going, but this is the road."

"He's waving you off this road," Khiry said.

"How do you know?"

"Look at him," Khiry said, gesturing toward the large, black dragon directly in their path. "He's pointing."

"Does he understand what he's doing?"

"Of course, he does. Stop! Stop before you run him over."

"Stars. Is he going to stand there while I run into him?"

Onyx hunched down and growled at Justin. Even though the guard had brought the jeep to a stop several yards from the dragon, Onyx made an impressive—and aggressive—display.

"He can make a point when he wants to," Khiry said. "Now you'll want to turn down this path." She looked to their right, trying to discern where the winding bend in the weeds led.

"That's not a path," Justin argued.

"It's something," she said.

"Look at it. That's barely more than a split in the brush."

"Yet more than the pine needles we're driving on now," Khiry argued. "Onyx is telling us to go this way for a reason."

"A dragon won't understand that this jeep can't go traipsing through the trees, you know."

"Please, for the love of God, just follow my dragon."

Within half an hour, Onyx had led the jeep and trailer into a clearing and onto a different path. While the trees around them still looked anemic, they grew further from the roadway.

More light reached the solar cell. It was apparent the colonists had maintained this corridor with some kind of blade followed by a heavy roller or mashing instrument.

Khiry smiled as they picked up the pace. Not only were they going to reach the secondary colony while they still had daylight, she now had reason to believe the people there continued to maintain powered vehicles. The roadway upon which they drove was flat, smooth, compacted, and recently made so.

Dr. Max called, "Tell Onyx my kidneys thank him!"

It took the better part of five hours to complete the drive to the secondary colony. Luckily, moving along this more structured road gave them better traction and better speed. As they neared the end of the hundred miles on the jeep's odometer, the road began to open into less forest and more cleared areas. For the last fifteen or so minutes of their journey, they could see the pouting volcano through the sparse canopy to the left of them. Then, the road turned, and the full effect of Vesuvius' rocky grandeur hit them.

The mountain towered about two kilometers above sea level, and it strained and stretched the dirt and boulders all the way to its summit. As if he had been pulling the continent up to his jagged lip for a century, the stretch marks of a Greek god gorging on rocks and sand for ages scarred the land for seven to eight kilometers.

Starting at the top, where heat wavered the dust in the air, the orange and black striations trailed all the way to the cluster of dirty, ashen clumps of society at the foothills where Justin had stopped at the edge of the choking forest. Green had months ago given way to brackish gray. This part of the world gagged on constant soot and heat.

As they approached, Onyx moved to the back of the party, giving Khiry and Kor the customary time to introduce the giant reptile as "friendly." The consideration turned out to be unnecessary. These people knew dragons — or scalers — could be allies. The secondary colony had dragons of their own.

Five pony-sized reptiles stood in a row, effectively blocking the path to the colony, not with size, but with presence. The five were varying shades of gray, tending toward the darker end of the spectrum, and all had the reptilian look of rock iguanas from Earth.

"Now why didn't Laino mention that," Khiry mused.

Kor grimaced, but none of the party pointed weapons at the line of small dragons behind three armed, masked colonists standing between them and the ramshackle clump of homes and tents. Beyond the homes and tents loomed the smoking mountain devoid of green.

It would have confused Khiry, would have put her back on Eldora as a child with Grammie Okie muttering something about diversity at last thanks to an overextended government, except for the lack of green.

Nothing here looked like it tried to survive any longer. Emaciated plants that would have emitted life-giving oxygen bent under the weight of embers that turned them from green to gray, as if in silent, final prayers. The trees that still had leaves hung heavy with death among the barren scene. Vesuvius had been breathing for himself, and nothing near him could survive the poison he exhaled.

The colonist standing in the center of the welcoming trio wore long pants that reminded Khiry of the blue jeans all her earthling crewmembers preferred. The other two appeared to have khaki pants similar to her own. All three of the guards wore long tunic shirts that flowed in an easy manner near their hips and thighs, pulling one's eyes down to their dusty boots.

Khiry wasn't sure why she expected these people to be as neat and tidy as the colonists at Laino Colony, but seeing their aged boots with cracks in them gave her a sense of their powerlessness. These people showed more bravado than they possessed. The center colonist lowered his fabric mask and spoke loudly to be heard clearly.

"Is that you, Justin Dreary? Haven't seen you up here for a couple years. I didn't believe it when a scout told me you'd found a giant phoenix to bring up here."

"We're not lookin' to cause any trouble," Justin half-shouted back, stepping out of the jeep. "We've got a landing party come to help."

He gestured to Khiry, who took that as her cue to slide out of the passenger seat. Mongoose moved with the speed and stealth of her nickname to Khiry's side. As if he understood the tension among them, Onyx trumpeted some kind of garbled stream of hoots and notes over all of them, and the five small dragons sat down. Dust rose and settled from the motion quickly, easily, as if no breeze could handle its weight.

Maubry made a show of wiping sweat off his brow with his sleeve to hide his grin and keep a laugh from busting out as the three colonist guards "got upset."

The man in the center, the one who had spoken so bravely a moment before, backed to the line of dragons, cursing and muttering and clearly asking one of the reptiles what was going on. The other two guards raised their weapons to point at nothing in particular, as they backed and scooted and danced around to the back of the dragon line.

Khiry turned to Onyx. "Really?"

The dragon shrugged his massive wing shoulders and sat down as well.

"What just happened?" Justin asked.

"This situation could use Electra," Khiry muttered. She placed her plasma gun in her waistband where everyone could see it, raised her hands to show they were empty, and began walking toward the dragon line with its dancing, scooting, confused colonist guards. Mongoose walked with her but didn't offer the courtesy of lowering her weapon.

Kor pointed to Justin. "Stay here." Then he pointed to Maubry and drew a line in the air to Dr. Max. "You, keep an eye on him."

As Khiry approached the line, she locked eyes with the darkest of the small dragons, entranced by her beautiful gray and deep-purple scales shimmering almost black despite the dusting of dross constantly descending. She smiled at the creature and addressed her first. "I don't mean to stare. I just can't help noticing how beautiful you are. You understand the human language this man uses?"

The creature nodded, her gentle slope of head and snout bobbing slightly down and then back up.

"He called you phoenix? Is that your species?"

The phoenix nodded again, blinking reptilian lids adorned with long, ash-laden lashes.

Khiry gestured with her head toward the party behind her. "My large friend back there is named Onyx, and his species is called dragon. You understood his language, too, didn't you?"

The phoenix nodded again.

"Can you communicate with him?"

The beautiful creature nodded once more.

"Would you be willing to do that? So we can make sure everyone is comfortable? So we can make sure everyone is safe?"

The phoenix stood and rastered like a bird to shake the embers from her scales and wings. With barely a sound, barely a print on the ground, she walked toward Onyx, her fluid, graceful body undulating with perfect movement and her long, sinuous tale held a mere inch from the dirt.

With that alliance in progress, Khiry looked to the main guard. Of course, he watched her cautiously, as she expected he would. She held out her hand to shake his.

"I'm Khiry Okerson, captain of the Coronado transport vessel."

He hesitated a second, and then took her hand. "Dan Heart. I don't really have a title."

"He's our leader," one of the others said. He lowered his mask to be understood better, and it revealed he wore a silly grin and overly red cheeks as he moved forward. The light stubble on his chin was flecked with gray whiskers to match his light hair flecked with gray at the temples, but those signs of age didn't take away from the flash and shine in his bright blue eyes. The man was genuinely pleased to introduce his leader—and himself.

"He's got a family here in the secondary colony and keeps us all in line, so we're well fed and safe. I'm Dexter. No family. I work in farming and I can fix anything that breaks around here. The phoenix you just spoke to is Hera. She's the alpha of the—"

"Dex," Dan interrupted. "She's the captain of a ship."

Kor cleared his throat. "Gentlemen, she's here to save your bacon, not help terraform."

The third guard chuckled from behind his mask. "You'll have to forgive Dex. We've been trapped on this rock for twenty-three years. He gets excited by a pretty lady."

Mongoose pressed a button that made her plasma weapon whine. It did nothing else. It merely made the weapon sound impressive. And it had the desired effect.

Dexter, and the phoenix nearest him, backed away from the newcomers.

"All right, now," Khiry said. "The point of this visit is to help you get away from that volcano."

Dan, the leader, began to laugh, but not with mirth. "In that little jeep?"

Dexter lost his flirtatious blush at that point. "There are children here we could put on the trailer to send back to a ship."

"To what end? Laino won't let a bunch of mixlings jump this planet." Dan looked at Khiry then. "Unless the Almighty Arbaseys Laino's dead, this trip of yours is a waste of precious time. Didn't anyone tell you why we're up here?" He looked over her shoulder at the rest of her away party. "Didn't Justin Dreary tell you why we're here?"

Khiry shook her head, because she now realized the reason they'd been given had been a lie.

"You're supposed to be studying the mineralogy," Kor provided.

Dan snorted and turned to walk away.

Dexter was more polite and spoke directly to Khiry. "Why don't you and your companions come to the center where we have stories and readings? We'll gather folks to talk. You can say your piece and figure if there's any point in taking the children back. It would be really nice if you could give the parents hope. Even if…even if there's no chance…"

He lowered his voice further, stepping closer to her: "It would be really nice for the parents to die thinking their children are getting off the planet."

CHAPTER SIXTEEN

The leader, Daniel Heart, brought a little more than a dozen colonists together in a hurry. Those who hadn't gone into hiding when Justin Dreary's approach was announced were easy to bring to the central building.

Khiry noted its utter lack of technology compared to the central hall back at the main colony. This one had basic wooden supports with tent material for walls. The mud and wattle roof currently supported a flock of birds picking at the mineral-rich mortar.

Dexter removed and waved his mask at the roof as the group approached, but the birds had no fear. They hopped and fluttered to the center of the roof to continue pecking at the dried mud between the woven twigs.

As she'd seen at the main colony, everything had a coating of gray sediment, but this area's layer was thicker. Here, the ash was ever-present in the air. Dr. Max had brought one of the boxes of surgical masks to the central building and opened it as soon as the group got inside. He began handing out masks to people as they came in.

One colonist after another dusted the cinders out of their hair as they stepped into the central tent, accepted a mask with a kind word or two, and stood off to the side to wait for their leader to share what was going on. Not everyone put forth the effort of donning a mask. Some already had fabric coverings they'd made from the same cotton-like material of their clothes.

Khiry noted how their clothes differed from the stretchy, polyester fabrics the citizens at Laino Colony had worn. These people moved with a heavy purpose under the drab-colored folds and flows of material that hid their features and strengths.

"Do you have any escape plan?" Khiry asked.

Dan shook his head. "We have a jeep similar to the one you came in on. Solar. It's what we take minerals to the main colony in. It's got a trailer like yours for carrying the load, but the trailer is busted beyond repair. I don't know if we can repair the jeep or not. A couple of the tech-minded among us have been working on it in between trying to keep everyone fed and keep the solar panels around here uncovered. The last big tremor from the volcano took out a set of caves where we had some food stores, the transportation." He paused. "Some other stuff."

"You're in triage mode," Dr. Max said.

"That's one way of putting it," Dan said. "Triage. And have been since the big tremor about two weeks ago. Three? Has it been three now?"

A few people nodded without speaking. The despair in the room couldn't be overstated.

"Then, a tremor yesterday morning did some more damage. How many people were you planning to take back with you?" Dan asked, looking directly at Justin.

The guard looked at Khiry, as if tossing the question to her.

She straightened her back and answered. "As many as we can. I want to find out what you can do to help with that. We have no idea what technology or information you have up here. If you're studying mineralogy, which I'm figuring out now is not the case, you'd have a pretty good idea what's in and around that volcano. What do you know? What sensors do you have?"

"Sensors?" another man piped up. "Are you asking if we have sensors to predict the future?"

Dan held up a hand to quieten the man before he got hysterical. "We had some sensors and controls that we salvaged out of a Panger cargo vessel—"

Justin gasped.

"Yeah, well, we don't need to keep a lot of secrets from the main colony anymore, do we? Like I was saying, we had some sensors that told us loud and clear this thing is about to blow, but those were wiped out when some boulders came rolling down the hill out there."

"We lost people, too," a woman snapped.

"She's asking what we know, Ming. Relax. We know this thing is going any day now. We also know there's no way we're getting the ninety of us back to the main colony and there's no way Laino's letting any of the pangerings off this planet. There'll be a fight first and we'll die by plasma cannon instead of ash and fire. Pick your poison."

Kor walked to the doorway to look up at the smoking mountain. "You salvaged stuff out of a Panger cargo vessel. Where's that vessel now?"

"Bottom of the ocean," Dan said.

Maubry groused, "That's no help then."

"We nearly lost Dex here getting what we could off it," the woman named Ming said. "But it's like sunken treasure now. Gone."

"How long ago was that?" Kor asked.

"Ten years?" Dan estimated. "Maybe eleven?"

"Was before my Callie had the triplets," a man offered. "Had to be at least ten."

Kor and Maubry exchanged glances. "No use."

"Tell me about the jeep, then," Khiry said.

"Busted the solar cell and a side of the engine," Dan said. "We've got the solar cell fixed. Good to go. The engine it powers, though…That's still a mess we haven't figured a way to fix."

Khiry pointed at Maubry.

"Hope it's in better shape than that old bugger at the other site," the engineer said.

The man who had spoken up about triplets and timelines hopped off a stone table. "I'll show you the cave it's in. I've been working on it in between shoveling soot."

Maubry clapped him on the shoulder as they moved to the tent flap. "Great. We'll get things moving. I brought lots of tools."

"If they can get that jeep to work, we can fancy up a new trailer, can't we?" Ming asked.

Dan shook his head. "We can try, but let's pray for one miracle at a time."

"How many kids are here?" Dr. Max asked.

"Seventeen," Ming said.

"Too many for your jeep alone," Dan said.

"We've got two nights and two full days left before we have to keep a good eye on that volcano," Kor said.

"That's what your sensors tell you?" Dexter asked.

"When we left Laino Colony this morning—"

Kor hesitated when Dan snorted.

"Frack Laino and his arrogance," Dan spat. "Not gonna save his skin, is it?"

"Uh, like I was saying, when we left the larger colony this morning, everything pointed to us having about seventy hours before pressure would get sketchy again. There's no reason to think that's some kind of countdown. We could be looking at more time to get out of here after that, but that's the window of safety we're working with right now."

"There's no reason to think that's a window of safety, either," Ming said quietly. "Is there?"

Kor didn't answer that.

Khiry looked out the tent wall opening that served as a window, watching Maubry and the mechanic talking engine rebuild strategy as they moved toward a specific cave nearby. She felt the weight of everyone's despondency pulling on her heart.

"I say we get the kids checked out," she spoke to the quiet room. "Let's gather some data. That'll give everyone something to do while Maubry works on the jeep for a couple hours. The parents can pack up some simple, easy-to-carry items while the kids are in here. Okay?"

Heads were nodding in agreement.

"Tonight, we get some sleep. In the morning, at first light, we drive the jeeps and kids back to the main colony. If sensors show we still have time, we'll get the jeeps back here same day, same path, fast as possible. One more night sleeping and then as many more as we can load on the jeeps get back to the main colony again. These phoenixes? They can fly?"

Heads were nodding again.

"Then they can get away. Can they carry a person?"

That question raised some eyebrows.

"*Would* they carry a person if they could?" Kor asked. "And how far could they get?"

Dr. Max shook his head. "It's a question of physics. These dragons, phoenixes, whatever they're called on this planet, their wings aren't large enough, their bodies aren't muscular enough to lift themselves and a full-grown adult. Especially not a full-grown pangering with the extra density, the extra organs and weight."

"And there are only six phoenixes that we know of," Dan interjected. "Or that we've met."

"There were five when we arrived," Mongoose said.

"There's a sixth one that has sort of bonded with one of the kids here," Dan said. "We call her Delta."

Dexter leaned close to Khiry and spoke to her specifically. "The phoenix," he clarified. "We call the phoenix Delta."

While Dan explained to the group that Delta was bonded to a child named Jillian and how the two had met, Khiry nodded to Dexter and asked, "Did the phoenix tell you her name?"

He chuckled. "I see why you're the captain. Smart like that."

"Maybe so," Khiry said. "But I want to know if these dragons can communicate in your language."

"They can. Surprised us, you know."

"Mmm."

"What are you thinking now?" Dexter asked, still in a conspiratorial tone.

"I'm thinking the dragon I met when we arrived here is very smart, too."

"Hera. Yeah, she's a smart one for sure."

"She let me believe she didn't speak," Khiry said. "It was my assumption, my ignorance, but she didn't know me, so she kept me in the dark." Khiry smiled to herself, impressed with the dragon outside the building. "Clever."

"That big dragon you travel with seems plenty clever," Dexter said.

"He is."

"Did you train him to do this diplomacy stuff with you?"

Khiry recognized the teasing lilt to the man's question and tightened her smile. Without being rude, she answered, "Surely, you understand a ship's captain has any number of diplomats traveling with her. I'm just lucky to have a dragon among them."

He bowed his head slightly, as if in deference to a member of royalty. "Lucky indeed. That dragon's twice the size of the phoenixes we have helping us. At least twice. I'd imagine he makes a good bodyguard as well as a nice diplomat."

"Well, even though I can protect myself just fine, I have a number of guards traveling with me as well."

As the colonists left the tent-like building, Kor stepped into Dexter's path and pulled him to the side. "Whose eyes do you have on?" he asked.

"I beg your pardon?" Dexter asked.

"You appear to be an older man," Kor pointed out the obvious. "I'm curious why you'd show the kind of attention you're showing to my captain, why you'd look at her the way you do."

Dexter frowned. "Why I look at her the way I do? She's a pretty young lady. I've been looking at the same women with untouchable daughters for twenty-three years."

"Then you understand the concept of this one being untouchable as well," Kor said.

"You consider the captain your property?" Dexter asked.

"She's no one's property. But she's at least three decades younger than you."

"I see. Your worry is an age difference?"

"That's only one of my worries," Kor said. "I could start ticking off a list, and at the top is you're supposed to be saving your people from a natural disaster, not looking for a teenager to flirt with."

Dexter hung his head. "I get it." He looked back at Kor, not smiling, but sort of grimacing at being schooled on behavior. "I get what you're saying. I'll keep my focus on getting off this rock."

While Kor had his man-to-man conversation with Dexter, Mongoose pulled Khiry aside. She quietly asked, "I have to ask, Captain, you know we can't fit these people on the Coronado, right?"

"I know."

"I'm not trying to question your orders or anything like that. I'm just worrying that we're piling up numbers we can't take on."

"I know," Khiry repeated. "The five hundred we talked to the other colony about won't work, so why add another hundred from here to the lottery, right? But I don't know what else to do. I'd rather give them hope…get them as far from this volcano as possible, as fast as possible. Maybe they can fashion some kind of boat…"

Mongoose rubbed her arm. "You're a good soul, Captain."

What Mongoose didn't say, but what Khiry heard in her own mind, was the truth of the matter. No boat fashioned out of any old ship panels would do any good. These people were destined for either a relatively fast death by fire, lava, and choking ash, or a slow death floating on an ocean with unknown dangers and no safe land for thousands of miles in any direction.

They'd seen it from space.

These people had nowhere to go.

*　*　*　*　*

As Dr. Max had requested of them, six sets of parents brought their kids to the central tent. "I'm so thankful you're willing to let us work with your daughter," Khiry said to one couple who lingered when dropping off a girl who appeared to be probably nine or ten, Khiry guessed. No good at judging ages, she would have guessed Lacy, back on the Coronado, was seven or eight, not ten.

"I can tell you want to help them," the mother said. She had introduced herself as Crystal, a doctor for this colony, and her husband as Rado, a hunter and builder. "I can tell it's genuine."

"It is," Khiry assured her. "Dr. Max just wants information first."

Crystal smiled kindly, the way a doctor should when speaking with a new patient. "Information and time?"

"We didn't want to be that transparent, but, yes. Time. Time to get the jeep fixed. Time to get things packed. Time to let folks around here relax and come to grips with the fact we're trying to help and…and…"

"And say goodbye," Crystal finished.

Khiry tried to smile, but she could feel her lips shaking slightly. She feared she was going to cry in front of this mother and father, so she shook her head slightly and said, "Perhaps goodbye or perhaps not. Look, maybe you can help me with something. Something that bothers me. I feel uncomfortable referring to your daughter as 'a mixling.' It feels as if I'm defining her as crossed between races, when she's…she's really a product of your love for each other.

"What term can we use to classify these children when we report back to USPS so we get a better word going in common use? So we get something standardized that sounds less mean? Less derogatory?"

Crystal pressed her glasses up on the bridge of her nose and said, "That's a lovely thought, Captain. But we don't care about that. Referring to Jillian as a mixling isn't an insult. It's what her DNA is. She's a mix of human alien and Panger alien." Crystal put her hand on Rado's arm where his long tunic shirt flowed past his elbow. "She's a mix of us."

"I can appreciate that. But people've been using it as a derogatory word for two decades, since before I was born."

"Then you have to lead the charge in changing it," Crystal said. "We don't necessarily have to stop using a word if it's correct. We have to change the use of the word to make it more correct."

"I agree with you. I hear you. I want to have people say only good words and not be mean and hateful in the way they speak to each other, but the fact is there are people out there in the galaxies, like Governor Laino, who snarl when they say 'mixling.' They make it sound like a mixling is a bad thing to be. How do we change a whole perception of a word when people use it like it's some kind of curse or plague?"

Crystal rested her head against Rado's muscular shoulder. While the woman's blue eyes practically shone with kindness and sincerity, Rado merely yawned.

"I'm afraid that's a question for the ages," Crystal said. "Some people are kind, like you. Some people are afraid of change, like Justin Dreary out there, who will go with whatever he's told to do to keep from losing his lifestyle. Some people are downright mean, like Governor Laino. He might accept that pangerings are part of our galaxy, just as earthlings are part of our galaxy, but he can't accept that they can love one another and form families, so he won't let anyone else accept that either.

"I know there are people in the Annady colony who don't approve of the blending of pangering and earthling, but they keep quiet about it because it's not their business. Then there are people in Annady colony who don't care one way or the other. And then…then there are people like Laino and Cass Hopely who can't accept the mixing and won't let anyone else accept it either. They feel the need to instruct others on how to live their lives. They aren't coming from a place of love. They're coming from a place of anger. A place of hardness. A place I can't understand."

Khiry got that. A place of hardness. She'd been in that place aboard the Instigator with Captain Marlon for nearly two years. The man had ranted and raved against anything that didn't conform to his ideals. She wondered if Marlon and Laino would have clashed or joined forces.

"I'll do what I can to change minds," Khiry said. "Or, better yet, to change hearts."

Crystal lifted her head from Rado's shoulder. "That's the banner. If you can convince people in their hearts to look on something with compassion, they'll be more likely to accept it with kindness, to change the way they talk about it, to change the way they think about it and react to it. Someday, the people on Earth and out here in the galaxies will understand that our mixling children are just children…just little boys and little girls…who want to grow up and be just people…young men and young women…like you and me."

Rado remained silent.

By this time, three more children who appeared to be four years old and seven more children who appeared to be ten or eleven years old had joined the others. In total, seventeen kids sat quietly along one side of the tent. Three were seated on the stone table where Dr. Max had asked them to climb up when they first came in.

Khiry glanced over them and said, "I think the faces here can help sway hearts."

"We should leave you to it," Crystal said. She nudged Rado's arm, signaling him to leave with her.

"You don't have to leave," Khiry said.

"It's all right. We know you have their best interest…"

Khiry tried not to stare at the woman's glistening eyes. It was obvious she fought emotion. Crystal wanted to leave the tent with its growing population of doomed children.

The space had been adequate for three adults and a teen a few moments before. As the children had come in and taken their seats in stoic, calm obedience, the space had become crowded with worry, crowded with anticipation of something not quite good.

"Of course," Khiry said. "We'll let you know when we've cleared your family for takeoff."

Khiry turned to Dr. Max, giving Crystal privacy to weep as she left the building. But when she turned to look over the kids again, Khiry noticed something similar about them. Or, rather, she noticed similarities in groups of them.

"What do you see here?" Dr. Max asked quietly.

"A lot of kids who look alike."

Dr. Max nodded once and turned back to the stone table where three children awaited their fate. The doctor smiled widely at them. "Kids! We're gonna do something fun!"

As Khiry knew he could do, he entertained the kids with silly word games and magic tricks to put them at ease while he collected a strand of hair with root attached, a mouth swab, a droplet of blood from a simple finger prick, and a jar full of laughter from each of them. She smiled at the way he clapped the jar's lid closed, as if something invisible to the eye would escape as each child finished a laugh into the metal canister he held in front of their mouths.

Each child leaving the building had a much better demeanor than when he or she entered. With smiles and a few giggles, they headed out in pairs or trios of uplifted spirits. Khiry waggled her fingers at them, wishing she could hand them a Zollipop™ like the doctors on Earth had done for her years and years ago.

It occurred to her that the non-sugary treat would have been like a Christmas present to these children. It would have been something so out of the norm that they would have gotten excited about it, despite the shadow cast over them by the ever-present pouting mountain. She wished she'd known, when she set out that morning, what this outpost would have in store for her so she could have brought treats and trinkets to brighten their otherwise gloomy outlook.

When the last set of triplets headed out with billowy—if somewhat threadbare—tunic-shirt tails brushing their legs, Dr. Max slipped into serious mode and began wiping microscope slides with dustings of powders, swipes of serums, and his tools of the trade. She paced while he worked.

"Do you want to check on Maubry's progress with the transportation?" he finally asked her.

"Ah, great idea," she murmured. "I'll be right back."

She practically skipped to the cave where she'd seen Maubry and the colony's mechanic walking earlier. She hoped her engineer's investigation of the jeep had gone well. The way Dan had spoken about the vehicle had given her a chill; she wanted to see how much damage it had sustained in the tremor he'd described. She could judge for herself what kind of timeline Maubry would be up against getting it ready for taking this number of kids back to the main colony where the Coronado waited.

In the old movies that humans had made for entertainment on Earth, spaceships and special vehicles always came together in the last minute. Bombs would be diffused with a mere second or two to spare. The hero always pulled the damsel off the tracks as the train sped by.

In the real world, timing doesn't work that way.

Khiry stood at the mouth of a cave looking at mangled parts and panels for a solar jeep that the secondary colony workers had been trying to fix for the better part of three weeks. Maubry glanced up from his box of tools that would not help, and then went back to leaning over the engine with the colony's mechanic. She didn't need to read her engineer's body language. She could see what a mess they had on their hands.

Her years traveling and working in her family's transport business had taught her the inner workings of a hundred different rovers and walk-abouts and jeeps of myriad power sources from solar to electric to hydraulic to combustion engine, and so on. This particular vehicle had been smashed by a chunk of boulder. It was bad luck. It was something an old Hollywood screenplay writer could fix, but a ship's engineer could not.

She walked calmly away from the cave, back to the building where Dr. Max moved slides on the microscope stage and made notes in his electronic tablet before making physical notes with pen and paper. The man was thorough. When he realized she'd returned, he motioned for her to sit next to him.

"This is extraordinary," he said. "These children are almost all related in one way or another. I find it difficult to believe the parents don't realize it."

"Do you think Laino was experimenting on these people? Is that the real reason they're out here, separated from the colony?"

"I don't know how to explain it, but there are common parents for certain. Common sets of parents. Per set of children. It's as if each mixed couple had multiple children per birth. Consistently."

"Then how are there only three mixlings back at the colony?"

Dr. Max cast a glance at her, then looked back into the microscope. "I doubt that's the case."

From the stone doorway, a small voice spoke softly, "My sister is back at the colony."

CHAPTER SEVENTEEN

Amid the scent of sweltering dirt mixed with ashen, sulfuric air, Khiry and Dr. Max invited Jillian to sit down and wipe her tears. The girl's blue eyes reminded Khiry of Crystal's kindness an hour before. This pretty child, a mere eight years old, already knew more prejudice and sorrow than most earthlings of the current age knew in their lifetimes.

"I can't say her name," Jillian said. "Sometimes Mom and Dad pray to the mercies for her safety, but they don't say her name. When I was born, I had a sister and a brother born, too. There were three of us. Mom says it was crazy hard, but she did it. We're not supposed to tell anyone about the three. We only talk about the two. There are two of us here and a mom and a dad."

"Your mom is Crystal? And your dad is Rado?" Dr. Max asked her.

"Yes. My brother is Jessup. I can't say my sister's name."

"Dexter told me you have a dragon friend," Khiry said.

"A dragon?"

"Um, not dragon," Khiry corrected herself. "Phoenix."

Jillian brightened a bit. "Yes, my phoenix is named Delta. She's so great. She's like having another sister, but one who's bigger than me and can breathe fire on stuff that would hurt me."

"Wow. She must protect you from all kinds of stuff," Khiry said.

"Yep. She doesn't let anyone tease me. And one time, when I was exploring the funny looking moths in the trees, she helped me get back home when it was getting too dark to see real well. It gets dark kinda fast here if you aren't paying attention. My mom was pretty mad about me being in the jungle, but Dad told her I have Panger eyes, even if they're Mom's color."

Khiry smiled at her. "Panger eyes do see better in the dark than human eyes. You're very lucky."

Jillian brightened more, her pink cheeks shining round and rosy. "I'm lucky to have a phoenix. I didn't want to make Dad mad, so I sure didn't talk back to him, but my eyes are normal. I don't see anything special in the dark."

"Sweetie, your eyes are normal for you, whether you can see like a pangering or like an earthling," Khiry told her. "Maybe it's just gonna take time for your eyes to adapt. Who knows when you'll get all the benefits of having Panger eyes?"

"I like that," Jillian decided.

"Do you and Delta play together all the time?"

"All the time," Jillian confirmed. "But we also do our chores. It's not *all* play and games. I'm growing into a big girl who can help in the colony."

"I'm sure you are. Did you get to play with your sister? Before she went to stay at the main colony?"

"Naw. Mom and Dad pretended she belonged to someone else who had a baby the very next day. That lady pretended she had two babies. Two earthling babies. That way, she will live like an earthling if something bad happens to us."

Khiry smoothed Jillian's hair and smiled at her. "I'm gonna make sure nothing bad happens to you, okay?"

"Okay."

Khiry and Dr. Max exchanged glances over Jillian's head. While she could already read the *be cautious* message in the doctor's expressions, Khiry couldn't yet read all of his thoughts as easily as she could read Devin's. She could guess, though. She could guess that this wise man would suggest she be careful not to promise something she couldn't guarantee. He would also suggest she not get too attached to a child she might not be able to protect.

While Dr. Max asked a few more questions about Jillian's health the past few years, Khiry figured she had discovered Trilby's younger friend, and she wondered briefly if the crew back at the Laino Colony had had any luck finding the eight-year-old sister-friend named Julia.

The math didn't make sense to her at first. The secondary colony had been created more than eight years ago. Crystal and Rado must have fallen in love after the others had been ostracized. The knowledge gave their love an even more tragic air in Khiry's mind.

It made them braver.

They had to know they'd get thrown to this technologically challenged outpost if anyone in the Laino Colony found out they were starting a family. It gave the woman who took in their third child some kind of sainthood in Khiry's eyes, and she wondered how she would go about finding the saint among six thousand people.

Of course, Khiry questioned her own motives. Was she planning to round up and evacuate all the mixling children? Or just the ones Laino had negatively impacted? She rubbed her eyes while Jillian chattered away with Dr. Max.

Maubry poked his head in the tent and said, "Hey, Captain. I think we have to call time of death on this engine. You wanna talk about Plan B?"

She sighed. "We better do that. Is Dan nearby?"

"On his way here right now. Got one of those little dragons with him."

CHAPTER EIGHTEEN

Daniel Heart walked toward the colony center with Onyx and the phoenix named Hera leading several of the colonists Khiry hadn't met yet. She invited Maubry in so he could share what he advised about transportation.

It didn't take long for him to explain what the colonists already suspected: The jeep was beyond repair.

"We're doomed, then," one of the men stated plainly, softly.

Maubry looked to Khiry in defeat. He didn't know how to respond to the sad but correct statement.

Khiry cleared her throat and stood a little taller next to Dr. Max. "I can't fit everyone on the Coronado. It's just not physically possible. But I'm trying to figure out a way to sneak the children aboard without…" She looked to Dan, as if the man could understand. "I'm trying to get the kids aboard without causing an uproar in the larger colony. I want to save as many children as I can. That's my goal."

Ming dropped to a rickety chair, weeping openly. "Thank the mercies," she sobbed into her hands. "Thank the mercies and graces and all that's good among the stars."

"All right," Dan interrupted. "Let's stay calm here and see what we can do. How can we help with this 'sneaking?' Are you suggesting the other colony won't want to save their children?"

"I'm suggesting the other colony doesn't know anything about this yet. They're planning to draw names out of a hat, and even that idea is problematic…it's too many. The ship is a cargo vessel. Look, I should start over.

"What I told you earlier about the Coronado is right. It's not a big ship. I believe we can get an extra fifty people aboard and reach another outpost before we use up all the air and scrubbers. But I'm afraid of making an announcement down in that colony like the one I'm making here. I don't trust Governor Laino and his elders. Justin here is making me nervous enough."

"Hey," Justin objected.

Dan held up a hand to keep Justin from continuing.

Instead, Khiry continued: "There are three mixling children from the Laino Colony who are aboard the Coronado right now under the pretense of research. Our other doctor is pretending to study them and send information to USPS with the idea that the information will cause USPS to speed up their rescue efforts if they think there's valuable mixling technology here."

"Wait a minute," Rado interrupted. "Your doctor is pretending to send research about an engineered race?"

Rado's words tickled the "paranoia" center of Khiry's brain, but she wanted to put her plan in motion. They didn't have time to stop and flesh out disturbing statements.

"Well, he's *going* to send the data. We're not lying to anyone. It's good, progressive information. And if it gets USPS off their collective butt, then it's a good ruse after all. We can hope Vesuvius holds off—"

"Vesuvius?" Dan interrupted.

"The volcano," Khiry supplied.

"Frack Laino and his arrogance. He named it Vesuvius?"

Khiry colored under the angry question. "I guess someone…someone in that colony did. But we can hope the volcano holds off until another ship gets here. But, to answer your question," she looked at the man who spoke of their doom, "I believe the majority of people on this planet are in trouble."

"But you're going to save our babies?" Ming said.

"That's my intent," Khiry said.

"How can we help do that?" Dan asked.

"I've been thinking that through," she said. She began to explain as a pair of colonists brought in platters of food for the group. A mix of root vegetables and almost ripe fruit piled high on each of four platters passed around the gathering.

While she spoke, she overheard a snippet of conversation from the corner; a colonist telling Mongoose, "We used to have fish, but the water's poisoning them close to shore."

"It's all timing at this point," Khiry said. "Kor told you that we've got two full days before things start getting wetter. If you like this plan, then here's what I suggest. We send Mongoose, Maubry, and Dr. Max back to the main colony with a group of kids at first light. Onyx can guide them to make sure they don't get lost."

"Wait. Why don't I just take them?" Justin asked.

"Because I don't trust you," Khiry stated bluntly.

Dan smirked at that.

"There'll be room for an extra child if I stay back with you," Dr. Max said.

"Thank you, Doctor, but I'm not done yet. The first group gets to the Laino Colony, drops everyone off at the Coronado. You take the kids aboard under the pretense of some kind of jungle fever that needs immediate attention. Maubry turns the jeep around and comes right back for the second group of kids. That means by tomorrow afternoon, close to sunset, the jeep with its trailer should be back. We sleep here again tomorrow night. Then, on the third day, Kor, Maubry, Justin, and myself take the second group of kids. And, of course, they have the same jungle fever that requires they be taken to the ship's infirmary."

"Contrived," Dan said. "I like it."

While the members of the colony started putting elements of her plan in motion, Khiry motioned to Dr. Max. "Could you single Crystal out? I want to talk to the two of you alone."

The doctor nodded, going into the small assembly to collect the woman. Kor looked to Khiry and asked, "Is there room for modifying your plan?"

"Why? What's wrong?"

"Nothing's wrong," he said. "I want to see the captain of the ship back with the ship as soon as possible."

"You want me to abandon these people in the morning."

He chuckled. "You know that's not what I'm saying."

"Of course. But I don't want them to think I'm escaping or something. Plus, there's something else going on here. Look at the way these people interact with one another. It's not like it was at the other colony."

Kor watched the handful of men and women, plus one horse-sized dragon, in the oversized tent, but wasn't seeing whatever his captain saw. "You spent a lot of time watching them," he said. "What's different here? What's making you uneasy?"

"I'm not sure yet. Maybe they're just careful and secretive because they've had to keep their kids and their lifestyle safe from the other colony."

"The other colony was that way. They were keeping this whole group of people a secret from us. Or trying to."

"Yessss," she agreed. "I can't quite put my finger on it."

While Khiry considered the secretive natures of both groups, Dr. Max led Crystal over to her.

"You have a question for me?" Crystal asked.

"Maybe a question, maybe a favor," Khiry said. "I don't want to alarm you, but Jillian told Dr. Max and me that she has—"

Crystal's suddenly widening eyes stopped Khiry short.

"No, no, there's a mistake," Crystal said.

"It's okay," Khiry said.

"We're not going to tell anyone," Dr. Max assured her.

"Should I excuse myself from this conversation?" Kor asked.

"No, you're a safe member of our group," Khiry said. "Look, there's no worry here. Trust me, Crystal. We know about an extra child, if you catch my drift, and I want to collect her to take off-world. But I'll need your help to find her in the other colony."

Crystal's obvious emotional swings were starting to attract attention that the lady didn't want. Dr. Max handed her a handkerchief from his pocket, which Khiry always found charming, and suggested, "Maybe we could have this conversation outside the tent, where it's quieter?"

The woman's nod couldn't have been any more emphatic. The trio helped the emotional woman step out of the tent and guided her to Onyx, who lay in a dust-heap nearby. He puffed his dragon cheeks to clear cinders from in front of his face as they approached and blinked the ash from his lashes.

Khiry patted his neck in empathy as Dr. Max spoke gently to Crystal and Kor took up a stance with his back to the little group. No one would bother them with the marksman standing guard like that.

"Jillian told us about a sister, but we already had suspicions because a friend of theirs is already aboard our ship."

Crystal dabbed her eyes with the handkerchief. "I can't believe it. Trilby. That silly girl went missing. Took her phoenix with her, thank God. That's the only reason her parents didn't lose their minds completely. They didn't come to the meetings we've been having. They've lost their will to even try at this point. You've got to tell them…at least…at least tell them she's safe."

"But not tell them what she was looking for?" Khiry asked.

"Right," Crystal murmured.

"Tell me why," Khiry prompted. "Tell me why you've hidden your other daughter among the Laino Colony if it's this dangerous."

Crystal shook her head slightly. "It's not rational. But we—Rado and I—thought Julia would have a chance that our other two children wouldn't have. If that madman down there ever got it in his head to wipe us out…"

Dr. Max and Khiry let the woman break down and pour out her tears. While she shook with sobs that had been hiding inside for eight long years, Khiry held her, gently patting her curly brown hair to comfort her. "There, there. We're going to help the best we can."

They gave her a few minutes to bring the sobs and hiccups under control while the dark and massive dragon behind them offered a cooing, purring sound. It resonated in their chests, bringing a strange calming vibration to their bones.

"I know where Julia is," Crystal said. "If Trilby had come to me…" She laughed a short, mirthless hiccup. "Well, I wouldn't have let her go into the wilderness looking for Jillian's long-lost sister if she'd come to me, and I'm sure she knew that. But, if you can safely get Julia to your ship…if you're willing…"

"Of course," Khiry said. "Yes. When the first jeepful of kids goes in the morning, you should be with them." She looked to Dr. Max. "Do you think we need an excuse to send her back? Do you think it's dangerous to explain the real reason to this group?"

Dr. Max grimaced. "We know we can't trust Justin Dreary, but he won't be going back yet."

"As the doctor here, I could go as a helper to you."

Dr. Max nodded. "Perfect."

"We'll make sure your son and you are on the jeep in the morning," Khiry said. She didn't know how to say they'd be stretching their luck to come up with an excuse to send Rado on the jeep as well.

Crystal smiled sadly. "I must say goodbye to my husband."

CHAPTER NINETEEN

Red and orange striations under a crust of black stretched toward the ocean on the west side of the mountain. The colors weaving under and among black rock, alternately glowing and hiding, would have been beautiful, if not for the portent of doom. Khiry watched its flow of raw, evil tentacles reaching ever toward the ocean as dusk gave way to night, and the people of the second colony gave in to resolve.

They would say goodbye to half their children in the morning. They were spending their final night as families. Caring friends shared the night with bereaved parents who would send their offspring with Maubry, Mongoose, Dr. Max, and Crystal to board the Coronado in the morning.

The mood pulled Khiry toward the core of the planet, giving her that sense of heaviness she'd felt when she'd first arrived, when she'd first stepped off the ship and this new gravity had influenced her body.

When she could stand the sight of distant lava no longer, she went into the central tent that was being set up for her crew to share until morning's light. One of the couples who had no children had invited Khiry and Mongoose to stay with them for the night. "You won't have to share quarters with all those men," they'd reasoned.

Khiry had thanked them for their kindness. "We can keep an eye on Justin in the tent," she'd said. Their thoughtfulness amid a colony's obvious pain and upcoming loss touched her, adding to the planet's gravitational pull on her.

Kor folded his jacket as he entered the tent. Khiry was offering some kind words to the last two colonists and he nodded to them, exchanging a calm, quiet "good night" as if they weren't all worried about saving seventeen young lives the next day.

He held the folded jacket out to Khiry as he pulled his mask from his face. "Pillow," he said.

She shook her head. "Thank you. I can use mine."

"Does the abundance of lanterns strike you as odd?" he asked.

"Not so much. They had torches everywhere down in the main colony. Must be getting the oil from somewhere on the planet."

He pushed forward his lower lip as he nodded, as if he accepted this reasoning. "Just seems like that governor down there would've kept all the fancy lanterns and such for himself."

"Maybe they're from here," she suggested.

"And Laino's taken the technology like he's taken everything else?"

"Exactly." She finished with a sneeze.

"Bless you."

"The ash is starting to get to me. I don't know how these folks can stand living in it."

"I bet they've grown used to it like the frog in gradual boiling water," he said.

"Sounds like something Dr. Max would say."

"I just saw him helping one of the phoenixes with the stuff around her snout."

"That's sweet," she said. She wondered if Onyx needed any such help. Would her large dragon friend need a mask of some sort to keep pollutants from traveling down into his lungs?

"Your voice just changed. Are you worrying about Onyx?" He patted the bench beside him to signal she should join him.

"I am. I'll feel better when he's back at the ship. Further from the volcano and closer to helping our crew. Nellie's big and strong and all, but Onyx can snap someone in half if they threaten El or anybody else."

Kor chuckled. "That's the truth. But when we headed out this morning, we had no reason to think the roadway would be as tricky as it was, would take so long, or that we'd need to hang out coming up with a strategy for evacuating a bunch of innocent kids over the next couple days. We didn't know we'd be here breathing this toxin for so long." He gave her a wink before saying, "With any luck, Onyx'll eat the governor when he gets back there tomorrow."

Khiry appreciated his attempt at levity. In fact, she watched his eyes shine in the lantern light, as if they sparkled specifically for her. As if he'd made the jest and awaited her reaction with that sparkle turned up to amused brightness only for her. She smiled to return his teasing: "If Nellie hasn't beaten him to the meal."

"There's my captain," Kor murmured, bringing his tone down an octave. He leaned toward her slightly. "And do you think El will have to help Nellie hide the bones?"

Khiry giggled at the playfulness of the awful question. "Only if those blasted spiders don't hide them up in a web somewhere."

"It pleases me when you laugh." As if Maubry and Mongoose entering the central tent and fiddling with tools and blankets on the far side of the enclosure could have interrupted them, he spoke lowly so only she could hear him. "I know this wretched planet doesn't lend itself to fun and games, but I look forward to our next adventure when you can laugh again."

She sighed deeply, letting a long breath carry weariness out of her. "I agree. An adventure where the people aren't in mortal danger."

"Maybe we should look for easy cargo to transport for an honest buyer."

She looked directly in his eyes, searching for a hint of sarcasm. He was being sincere, and she liked that. "Agreed, again. The honest traders might not pay as well as the mercenaries…"

He nodded. "The Badlar Intergents of the universe?"

She grinned at the memory of a tradesman who had brought trunks of stolen tapestries aboard the Coronado before they'd left Pangaea Moon not long ago. The man had been one of many who'd succumbed to a plague that could best be described as "zombies" aboard the ship. Her crew had sold the tapestries on Earth while she and Electra were in the Wascana.

"Well, whatever the honest traders are willing to pay, we've got plenty of room in the cargo hold to pack the Coronado with legal merchandise for a good day's wages," he reasoned. "Between you and Electra Endh, I've no doubt we can negotiate fair terms and get a few lucrative paydays under our belts before we return to our life of crime and running from USPS."

Willing to put their current situation to the back of her mind for a few minutes longer, she laughed lightly at his summary of their past three months. "Our life of crime and running from USPS wasn't even our fault," she said. "Yet it feels as if we keep trying to get back our good name. Even here on this planet. What are we doing? Are we trying to save these people? Or are we trying to stay in USPS's good graces?"

"I don't want to sound like Frederick the Conspiracy Theorist, but we might be putting ourselves *out* of USPS favor by taking five hundred people off this planet. Five hundred or however many we can get back for. I get the impression these people were left here to die."

She looked at her hands on her lap. "I think you're right. It worries me that no one responded after their last communication to Earth. It worries me that someone gave the order to destroy the Eleos. It worries me…"

"That these people were left to suffocate under an ash cloud?" he finished for her.

"Or worse."

"I can't imagine what would be worse than suffocating to death," he mused.

"I don't want to think about it." She involuntarily shuddered and took a deep breath. As if her body wanted to confirm she could still breathe in and out, she did so. She looked back into his eyes, his eyes that watched her soulfully.

"How could I survive if I wasn't breathing your air?" he asked.

It seemed an overly romantic sentiment coming from her marksman, her weapons specialist, her ship's trained killer. Hers. She smiled at the thought.

Hers.

"I hope that smile's a good sign," he said, tucking a wisp of her hair behind her ear.

"Yes, a good sign," she answered.

"I want to provide for you," he said. "And I don't mean just here, bringing in the vegetables these nice people gave us for supper. I want to make sure you're always safe and always have what you need to succeed out here in these galaxies."

"I think you already do that," she said. "I'm only keeping it together because you and Electra are at my side. You two are my support."

He nodded at that. "Good. Good. But you know you can turn to me, right? I'm here…"

She let the color and heat rising to her cheeks give her answer because she wasn't sure what words were the right ones to say. How should she tell this man that she already considered him vital to her existence? Would he see that as a weakness or a strength?

"Captain," Dr. Max said gently from the tent's doorway.

Khiry realized then that Maubry and Mongoose had stopped moving tools and weapons around. Justin Dreary had taken a reclining position under the table where Dr. Max had examined the children earlier that day. And Dr. Max stood in the doorway, with Jillian and her phoenix's head looming over her.

"Yes?"

"Jillian and Delta would like to join our crew for the night."

Mongoose laughed from the other side of the tent. "That sounds like a slumber party from Earth!"

Maubry looked to Kor and mouthed the question, "Slumber party?"

"Oh, my, I'm not sure Delta will fit in here with all us people," Khiry said. "Let's give it a try."

As if the mini dragon had been waiting for that permission, she hooted once and pushed Jillian into the tent ahead of her.

CHAPTER TWENTY

Tempel Pliny recognized his mistake as soon as he saw a caged, misshapen bag wriggling.

The crewmembers had given him a wide berth to roam freely around the Coronado; no one stopped him from going to the brig. They basically ignored him because they trusted their young captain implicitly. When she informed the crew that Tempel, as Annady's official historian and record keeper, would be uploading documents and images from the past twenty-three years to the ship's bibliotecha, each crewmember accepted that task on its face. Each person he encountered in the dimly lit corridors nodded or smiled — or both. One fellow asked if he needed help finding a computer station.

Of course, Tempel didn't know Electra monitored his onboard activity from the bridge. She watched for system bugs and computer viruses that might be a little less obvious than a bag of spiders, but possibly more insidious. To her astonishment, the only "spyware" his software installed was to re-route controls from the bridge to engineering when a wristplate device activated a specific trigger. No doubt that would be for Laino to take over the ship once they were in deep space.

She waited for Tempel to disengage the palm-size computer pad he'd carried aboard before re-routing the code and controls. Jevron worked with her and the two soon had the system in place to give any mutineers a two- or three-second false sense of power. And then the Coronado crew would be back in charge.

Jevron returned to hunting spiders with his team and Electra returned to watching Tempel.

The latter moved toward his next goal — the brig, of all places — thinking his governor's plan took perfect shape. His task in the brig was to change codes so Laurel Eidon could override the young security chief's commands there.

In Tempel's mind, he considered it perfectly logical that members of the Coronado's crew would balk at Governor Laino taking over the ship; they'd need to be confined to a cell or two during the journey to Earth. It would be in everyone's best interest to lock the senior staff in the brig with codes none of them were familiar with.

When Tempel whooshed open the sliding door to the brig, a rancid smell rushed out, overtaking the pleasant, spicy smell that had hung on the air until then. He scrunched up his nose and shook his head violently against the stink of death. Had the crew left someone to die in the brig? Surely not. None of the officers had come across as cruel.

*　*　*　*　*

On the bridge, Electra frowned at the console before her. "Why's he going to the brig?"

Lacy and Trilby sat nearby, happily draping scarves around Junior's dragon neck. He practically panted with joy at their attentions. Goldie slept in a curled mound of dragon scales at the front of the bridge, soaking up the sunshine like a cat from Earth.

"Are you still watching Tempel Pliny?" Trilby asked.

"I am."

"My mom said he's one of those historians that writes what the winners want him to write."

Electra smirked. She understood what the girl had difficulty expressing; the documents, stories, and pictures Tempel might have uploaded to their bibliotecha should be taken with a grain of salt.

Then Electra's smirk disappeared. "Did he release Frederick?" she asked herself. "How did he know Frederick was in there?"

She flipped a comm link to connect to Jevron, who was back to leading "operation spider annihilation" duty.

"Jevron, this is Electra."

"Go ahead, Electra."

"I need you to check on our prisoner in the brig. I think Frederick's been released."

"Released? I'm a couple hallways from there. I'll check right now."

She switched the link to "off" and reached to bring the brig camera online. It failed. Then she noticed the temperature in that room was more than a sweltering thirty-three degrees Celsius.

"Oh, this is not dry," she muttered.

She flipped the comm link to the brig and shouted, "Tempel! Get out of there now!"

*   *   *   *   *

With the initial blast of stink dissipating in the hall around and behind him, Tempel stepped into the overly warm room of metal floor and metal bars. The dim light reminded him of the abandoned houses on the outskirts of Laino Colony. The smell reminded him of decaying meat. And the wiggling, odd-shaped sack in the nearest cell reminded him of a cocoon.

As he stepped slowly, cautiously toward the cell with its human-size bag of gurgling, crinkling movement, he realized he stared at not a sack, but at a series of webs.

And thousands of legs.

Above his shriek, he heard the "chunk" of a comm link engaging and Electra Endh shouting, "Tempel! Get out of there now!"

He didn't have time to comply.

142

The legs erupted from the crinkling web, unentangling in a massive rush of pointy talons and one-inch fangs attached to hand-size spiders. The hairy creatures moved as if signaled by Tempel's beating heart. And when his heart rate shot into the stratosphere, more of the spiders answered the call, dropping from the brig ceiling and scurrying with a flurry of hair and feet from every corner and crevice.

He was overcome with the crawling, jumping, biting creatures within a second of Electra's warning. He fell in a flailing, screaming mass, trying to roll away from certain, painful death.

Jevron was running toward the screams as they became a garbled, lower-volume, hoarse cry behind legs and hair descending Tempel's throat. When Jevron slid to a stop in the brig doorway, he tapped his comm device at his ear and shouted, "El! Fire! Close brig door and burn it down!"

He started the blaze with a quick flamethrower burst as the door whooshed closed.

CHAPTER TWENTY-ONE

Khiry hugged Mongoose before the security chief climbed onto the jeep's trailer with Dr. Max and a few kids. Maubry held his fist up in the air from the driver's seat. "I'll be back this afternoon, Captain."

Onyx trumpeted his agreement with the engineer, while Kor adjusted a set of ropes that a child would use to hang onto the dragon's neck.

Khiry couldn't stand the sadness radiating off the colonists around her. She wanted to change everything happening. Wanted to bring the Coronado to this spot, load up all these colonists, and take off for Pangaea Moon, as if no interruption in their plans had brought them to this horrible planet of doom.

But it was too late for such things. Lifting from the ground beside Laino Colony would send all manner of terror into the people there. Her senior staff couldn't decide to save ninety people here and leave six thousand in the colony to the south.

Watching the jeep crunch and roll into the choked and graying cypress trees toward the main colony, she allowed a sense of foreboding to wash over her.

"At least those will be safe," she muttered.

Jillian looked up at her. "He's bringing the jeep back for more of us later today."

As a true leader should, Khiry mustered a smile to reassure the child. "Yes, yes, he is."

* * * * *

Electra spent the morning cleaning webs out of the panel under the communications console on the bridge. When she felt confident no hairy, eight-legged monstrosities would drop onto her face, she lay on her back to get a better angle to reach into the paneling and wipe at the wires. Adam Okerson handed her swabs and accepted the disgusting, web-coated ones as she worked.

"Khiry would have a fit if she knew those things had gotten to the bridge," Adam said.

"Agreed."

"Even as a little kid, she didn't like the creepy crawly things that got on board from some of the cargo we hauled around."

"Can't blame her there," Electra said. "These spiders have caused no end of trouble with the comms. I can't understand why they've targeted. *If* they've targeted. It makes no sense."

"You think USPS engineered them to fix on our communications?"

Electra moved her head to peer out at Adam. "I hadn't thought that before. But now that you say it…it freaks me out a little bit."

He shrugged. "I don't trust the government, you know."

She went back to scraping sticky stuff off wiring. "I know."

They both turned their attention to someone clomping up the metal steps outside the bridge then. Mongoose shouted in to them: "El! Maubry and I brought some people back with us!"

"Sounds like you get to finish this," Electra said. "I know you've traveled space all your life and handled many a ship. Are communications systems among your expertise? Can you clean this mess in here without damaging anything vital?"

"Thank you for asking that like I'm *not* an idiot," he said. "You're so much nicer to work with than my older sister or my dad was. Yeah, I can do this and get us back online."

Electra crawled out from under the console and handed him the clean swab she held. With a wink, she said, "that's why Khiry keeps me around. I don't offend people."

He snorted a laugh while he took her place on the floor. She greeted Mongoose in the bridge doorway.

"Who are we bringing onboard?"

"You won't believe this, but it's a bunch of kids."

"And a doctor," Dr. Max called from the base of the steps behind them. "Electra, can you send Lacy and Trilby to the infirmary? I'm going to treat that as home base for the next hour or so while I get everyone settled in."

Electra peered into the cargo hold where a group of eight children and a woman she didn't recognize corralled a small dragon, similar in size to Goldie, toward the stairs leading to the infirmary.

"Our comms are down all over the ship, so I'll need to go find them," Electra said. "That's not a problem, though. I think Chef Holly was teaching them how to make donuts in the galley."

"Ooo, I like donuts," Mongoose said under her breath. "I can go get them for you."

Electra grinned at her. "Go for it."

"But tell me about this comms situation first," Mongoose said. "What's happened?"

"Those stupid spiders. Every time we think we have them beat; we find a clutter of them behind a panel somewhere. They keep screwing up the wiring in the comms."

"That's not very dry," Mongoose said. "Anything else affected?"

"No. And that's what's strange. Adam and I were just talking about it. It's like they're targeting our communications systems."

"I don't like that," Mongoose said. "You think they're intelligent? Doing it on purpose?"

"Only when I get that paranoid feeling."

Mongoose pointed at her. "You're not paranoid if people really are trying to spang you from the heavens."

Maubry stepped from the ramp into the cargo hold below and stood with his hands on his hips. He scrunched up his nose. "Why does it smell like fire? What's been on fire?"

"Oh, yeah, we had an incident with the spiders and one of the colonists," Electra said.

Maubry looked up at her and Mongoose. "What's that? Can't hear you for all these kids," he teased them.

The children pretended to appreciate his light-hearted fun. Their somber shuffling toward the back of the cargo hold wasn't raucous by any means. Maubry's insincere complaint was meant to lighten their spirits somewhat…somehow…

"I'll fill you in on the fire we had," Electra said. "It was in the brig. All solved now."

Mongoose frowned. "Where's Jevron? I left him in charge."

"He's doing a fine job," Electra said. "He's the one who used the fire to solve the problem." She lowered her voice to say, "These kids look depressed. What's happened? Is Khiry back?"

"I wish. She'll be back tomorrow. Maubry's going back for her and another load of kids from the other colony as soon as he gets the jeep prepped for the return trip. It's pretty sad. There are about ninety people at the other colony, stranded with no means of transportation other than our jeep."

"Ours? What about the hovercraft in Laino Colony? They've got solar powered vehicles."

"If you can get that governor to lend them to us, I'd be surprised, but I'd also say that's a good plan. Can you talk to him?"

Electra nodded. "Let's do one thing at a time. If you get Lacy and Trilby to the infirmary for Dr. Max, I'll get myself cleaned up to go see the governor. When's Maubry headed back?"

"Ah, I think right away. Maubry?"

He looked up from a young lad he was helping with a face mask. "Yes?"

"When are you going back?"

"As soon as possible. I gotta get there before dusk."

"Makes sense. Electra's gonna see if Laino will let us take a couple of their solar jeeps."

Maubry muttered something the ladies couldn't hear, and the lad in front of him looked sadly at his face. "But shouldn't you still try?"

Maubry considered that for a second. Chagrined, he put a hand on the lad's head. "You're right. Of course, you're right. We have to try, even if that old man is stubborn and cruel, we might be able to turn his heart in light of the scary times we're coming into. It's worth a try."

* * * * *

At the Laino Colony that afternoon, Laurel approached the main hall carefully. "Governor, their jeep has returned, but…" Laurel's voice faded, as if he waited for reproach. His leader had plenty of reason to turn on him at the moment.

Governor Arbesys Laino patted Donna's head. He stood facing the child, one hand on her shoulder, so frail beneath the tight leotard he'd asked the ladies to stain a berry pink for her. He gave this youngling everything he could think of to make her life better, to make her passage through this universe an easier one.

Everything except freedom.

"But, what?" Laino asked.

"But they brought back the north colony's doctor, who went into the city with their security chief. I didn't have enough warning to have them followed. I have no idea what they were trying to learn."

Laino placed a flower wreath on the child in front of him, as if crowning her. "You haven't failed us, Laurel. Tempel will have hidden any medical records that are sensitive."

"Also, Electra Endh has come to speak with you."

Laino raised his line of bushy eyebrows in surprise. "Is her captain with her?" He emphasized the word "captain" sarcastically.

"No, sir. She's alone. She's waiting just outside the hall. Dressed in a USPS uniform."

Laino smirked, still staring at the child in front of him, still touching her face with one hand as if he knew he said goodbye this afternoon.

"Does her uniform disturb you?" Laino asked. "You act like you're disturbed."

"Well, sir, their engineer has brought a group of children with the other colony's doctor back to their ship."

Laino frowned.

"Children and a scaler," Laurel clarified,

"This makes no sense. Why would they seek to imprison another scaler? Is it alive?"

"It is."

"Is this one injured like the last one?"

"It doesn't appear to be. It flew of its own volition. Alongside that big dragon they have."

The governor sighed deeply. "It won't matter when we take the ship. We'll toss the scalers and any mixlings off before we jump the planet. Is Tempel aboard?"

"He is. Their captain gave him permission before she left, and he's been aboard since early this morning. I've not received any messages from him yet, but the palm drives he took were easily explained—"

"Good, good," Laino interrupted. He knew how the plan was to come together; he didn't need Laurel to bore him with it now. "Would you send Cassidy in to update me on the lottery? It seems to be taking her a long time to organize how to pull the correct names in front of everyone."

"Of course, Governor."

"And you can send Electra Endh in as you go. My curiosity is piqued."

Laurel didn't leave, though. He stopped at the sensation of the floor shaking and grabbed hold of the table in the center of the room. The two men's eyes met for a moment, and Laino shoved Donna toward the door. "Run to your mother, Girl. Quickly. Get home."

CHAPTER TWENTY-TWO

Early afternoon found Khiry helping a group of colonists push a coverstone into position upon a set of angled boards. The colonists had chiseled the opening of a cavern into a curve that matched the inner ridge of the coverstone beautifully. It would cap their hiding place when Vesuvius erupted.

When the stone lay in place, and a few of the men clapped each other on the back in congratulations of a task well done, she used her fabric mask to wipe her brow and went in search of another job to keep her busy. Kor appeared to be working with a pair of phoenixes to stack rocks and mortar on the outskirts of the little town, at the top of a hill. A group of women carried supplies to a tent on the far side of the rock wall. Grabbing a sack of turnips or some kind of root vegetable, Khiry made her way up the hill.

"Captain!" Jillian greeted her. The child had mortar on her hands and smudging along one of her cheeks.

"Wow, it looks like you're helping build a wall," Khiry said.

From behind the wall, Delta popped her head up as if to remind them she was helping as well. The phoenix's deep blue scales had mortar complimenting the gray cinders today.

"And Delta's helping, too."

Jillian grinned. "My dad said I might as well be useful while I'm still here."

"He's smart to add your hands to the labor," Khiry said. "You look like a good worker."

The girl beamed under the praise.

Kor stabbed his trowel into the bucket of mortar at their feet and announced, "We need more stones. Delta, will you help me bring more up here?"

Another man nearby spoke up as well, "I can help bring more, too."

As a woman accepted the bag of vegetables from Khiry's arms, a rumbling grumble reached their ears and then their feet. "Do you feel…" the woman began asking.

She didn't finish her question.

Vesuvius growled with a rolling, building thunder, louder than the screams and shouts of colonists around the various work sites. Jillian grabbed Khiry's hand, the instinct to reach for a mother figure overtaking the child. Both Khiry and Kor looked up at the vomiting mouth of the mountain and then back to each other.

"Run!" he shouted, his pointing toward the south unnecessary.

For some reason, colonists ran toward the southwest, toward the ocean Vesuvius had been drooling poison into for weeks. Kor directed Khiry and Jillian inland, away from the caustic waters no one would reach before lava caught up to them.

* * * * *

When Vesuvius spat his plume of ash and pyroclastic doom into the sky, Maubry had already traveled half-way to the secondary colony. He felt the tremor before he saw the streaks of fire and smoke in the sky above the canopy. He knew what was happening and pushed the jeep to go faster.

At the ship outside Laino Colony, Crystal looked to Dr. Max and Devin in the infirmary with terror. "Oh no. It's early. It's too soon."

It took them all of a minute to realize Maubry couldn't have reached the secondary colony yet; the kids to the north wouldn't be on their way to safety. Crystal couldn't hide her agitation. "Electra went to get a hovercraft from the governor? Is that right? Has she returned? Can I take it —"

"I'll do you one better," Devin said. "You ever ride a dragon?"

Nellie seemed to understand immediately what the humans wanted and lowered her belly to the ground to facilitate Crystal climbing onto her back. Onyx trumpeted a blast alongside them and rose into the sky first, beating his magnificent black wings like sails demanding the wind do his bidding. He led Nellie in the path Maubry had taken.

CHAPTER TWENTY-THREE

Khiry emitted a shriek of horror mixed with remorse as she ran full tilt, with Jillian struggling to keep up. She had a grip on the child's hand that rushing rapids couldn't have dislodged; she couldn't stop to help a man who stumbled into blackness when a fiery rock pelted him on the head. She couldn't stop to help a woman who tumbled headlong toward a flowing river of glowing orange fire to the side of the hill they ran along.

She soon realized the tears stinging her eyes blocked as much sight as the roiling embers surrounding her. And she was thankful not to see the flaming rocks Vesuvius threw in his rage. She was thankful not to see people dying in the darkening smoke.

"You can run faster, Jillian," Kor shouted encouragement.

There came a point as they ran when Khiry realized he was wrong. Jillian was part pangering, and within her body lay certain strengths. And within her body lay heavier organs that were sapping her strength now.

Kor must have come to the same conclusion because he took advantage of a natural stacking of rock and boulders near their path. He pulled Khiry and Jillian behind the outcropping as a rush of rolling smoke caught up to their feet.

Delta landed beside them, lifting her snout to trumpet a wail of despair. Jillian buried her face in Khiry's shoulder, sobbing and coughing amid gasps for heavy breaths.

"This crap is climbing the hill," Kor spoke into Khiry's hair. "And it's climbing fast. I don't think we can outrun it."

Khiry pulled Jillian to her breast, hugging the crying child to comfort her. "I don't know what to do."

"Delta can get out of here," Kor said.

"She's too small to carry us," Khiry shouted above the crashing and smashing of boulders.

Kor coughed and heaved dust from his lungs as he bent over to rest his hands on his thighs. Khiry knew this was the end.

This was it.

This was death.

"But she can carry Jillian!" Khiry shouted.

Kor watched her while he coughed, still sputtering from the effort of running as hard as they had been. He watched Khiry place a kiss on the mixling child's cheek before she threw Jillian onto the phoenix's back.

"Hold on tight!"

Khiry's hair had come loose from her ponytail, so he couldn't see her face, couldn't see that she was crying. But he could see her placing Jillian's arms around Delta's neck. The phoenix wailed again, as Khiry stroked a hand down her neck and another hand down a wing.

"Fly, Delta! Fly!"

The creature wailed and screeched a sorrowful, horrible cry as she beat her wings against the air, lifting twice her normal weight up into the darkening sky, up above the hot, roaring ash clouds.

Khiry turned to Kor, shaking. Her whole body trembled.

This wasn't fair.

The heat and embers were still coming for them. Behind the shelter of the boulder, their death would take longer than out in the open.

He pulled her to him and stepped away from the shelter, back to the open, back to the field where the lava and pyroclastic flame rocketed toward them. Thank God the flames and burning were somewhere under the black boiling clouds where they couldn't see it. They wouldn't know death had reached them until it was too late.

She stepped into his embrace and looked up into his eyes. Those deep brown eyes she'd wanted to stare into for the rest of eternity in space. As he brought his lips to hers, the trumpeting of a dragon called to them.

"Oh, God," she sobbed against his lips.

"Onyx," he whispered back.

Up from the black clouds that turned and churned toward them, Onyx flew like a torpedo from the Coronado's weapons bay. The mighty dragon hurtled toward them with a speed that could rival any spaceship she'd ever piloted.

He didn't slow as he swooped but opened his claws and grabbed them by their torsos, yanking them from heating ground as the lava tried to lick their boots.

Khiry's stomach lurched as Onyx rose above the reaching clouds of heat and black. She gripped a hard, scaled bone that felt like Onyx's talons, holding it tight at her breast, and screamed some unintelligible shout of exultation and terror all in one. Bile threatened to choke her as she shrieked, and she swallowed sound and gore as they flew.

Flew over emaciated trees falling under the river of lava.

Flew toward the Laino Colony to the south.

CHAPTER TWENTY-FOUR

Nellie and Crystal had found Maubry walking back toward the Coronado. Despondent, the pangering had nearly cried when he saw them approach and land near him.

"One of those rocks smashed the solar cell," he said. "Smashed it. There was nothing I could do."

Being a doctor, Crystal recognized hysteria brought on by the traumatic experience. She had him sit on a broken tree and offered him kind words. She checked his blood pressure and let him ramble out the story in broken sentences and obvious shock until he finally slowed the stream of worry and anger.

Until he finally cried at having failed his mission.

Until he finally realized he sat with the mother of one of the children he hadn't saved.

"I'm so sorry," he finally said.

Crystal fought back her own tears. "We're gonna make it out of this somehow. You can't blame yourself for a volcano erupting too soon. Nellie here can fly us up there to see if there's any hope."

By the time Nellie had carried a human and a heavy pangering another few dozen miles toward the secondary colony, they realized they were seeing devastation that no one could survive. No one on the ground would be alive to save. And so, Nellie made the long flight back to the ship, stopping to rest near the damaged jeep so they could salvage pieces from it. The lovely dragon waited patiently, calmly, quietly, while human and pangering worked together, neither aware that relief awaited them back at the ship.

* * * * *

"I realize you've had a near-death experience," Laino said, insincerity oozing from his lips. "But you can't take time away from your duties to dwell on your feelings."

Khiry put her hand on Devin's arm to keep the doctor from answering curtly. Instead, she raised her chin higher and said, "Governor, I've given you as much respect as I can muster considering you left nearly one hundred of your people to die—"

"How dare you!"

"Let me finish. Governor, you have been uncaring regarding the people at the base of that mountain and now they're—" Her voice caught in her throat, making the next few syllables difficult to get out. "—incinerated by lava or suffocated by heat. I'm appalled that you haven't even pretended to care."

"We haven't the luxury of time to mourn them," he snapped. "Has it occurred to you that I'm trying to convince you to save the people right here in front of you?"

"Has it occurred to you that I don't believe a word coming out of your mouth?"

Laino glowered at her for a moment, as if considering what he could and couldn't get away with saying at this point. He glanced at Kor's hand resting on the plasma gun at his belt.

"All right," Laino finally said, as if conceding the argument. "I recognize my leadership style is foreign to you. I recognize I haven't taken the time to explain myself to you. I recognize my fear and concern for my citizens has made me appear aloof, when, in fact, my only goal is to get as many of my people off this planet as quickly as possible. And that has been my only goal since the first communiqué was sent to Earth three months ago.

"I apologize that you've not been given better information and haven't had a chance to see my clear motives to save my people. Now, please, can we go, together, to the central hall and read off the names that Cassidy has pulled from the lottery so these people can finalize their preparations tonight? Why are you shaking your head? Why is this not acceptable?"

"I believe reading the names and having people immediately board as their names are called will be the safest way to maintain calm and orderly boarding and we can do that in the morning before lift-off."

"All right," he said again. "You want to keep all of my people in suspense for another night."

"I want to keep everyone calm for another night. I can't imagine the chaos or unrest we might be inciting if we single out five hundred people this evening, and then the rest know they'll have to wait. If your name wasn't called, wouldn't you go mad knowing you had to stay here and wait for the ship to come back weeks from now?"

He sighed deeply, as if he had, once again, to admit she had a point.

"Are you absolutely certain the old transport vessel won't work?" she asked.

He closed his eyes, as if steeling himself against rage. "I am. Absolutely. Certain."

"God, I'm sorry to hear it," she said. And she meant it. "Let me think on more options for getting as many of your people to safety as possible. I want to sleep. I want to keep our spider problem from getting off the ship—"

"Spider problem?"

"It's a long story," she said. "Let's meet again in the morning."

"At the central hall," he said.

She nodded. "Yes. At the central hall."

Laino pursed his lips before saying, "I will make the arrangements."

As the elder walked away, Devin looked at Khiry with skepticism. "He could have said thank you."

"He has other plans," Kor said.

"We'll have to talk about this again in the morning," Khiry lied. Neither man noticed the shine had gone out of her doe-brown eyes. At least, neither of them commented on it.

"Were you being serious when you told him you wanted to sleep on it?" Devin asked.

"Yes, I was being serious. I want our crew back on the ship and the cargo bay door closed for the night."

"Whoa," Kor said. "You don't trust them at all."

"No, I don't. And I need to keep our people safe while we make some decisions."

"These are hard decisions," Devin said.

She didn't know how to respond to that. He was right. But his statement also reminded her that the hard decisions belonged in one place. On her shoulders. Considering the pride she'd nurtured in her heart the past few weeks, it was time to own up to her role as captain. The tough decisions with the harsh consequences didn't belong on the shoulders of the crew following her.

"Devin," she said softly, "would you get back to the ship and let the crew know that we'll have a meeting before we go to the central hall in the morning? There's no way we'll fit five hundred people and their belongings on board. We'll have to figure something out. Everyone should get a good night's rest in preparation."

"Of course, Captain."

CHAPTER TWENTY-FIVE

Khiry and Kor had been quietly resting against the boulder for about half an hour after Nellie and Crystal brought a bruised and thankful engineer back to the main colony. No one wanted to speak of the terrible loss of life to the north. It was easier to push that hurt and pain down deep in the pits of their stomachs and bury their feelings in work; they had to prepare to leave before the next big blow.

The sunset hidden behind clouds of creeping ash brought memories of wars on Earth. Khiry found herself pretending to be content with the quiet conversation, the tender conversation balanced with deep discussions of life and death.

She'd served with Kor for two years aboard the Instigator without admitting to herself how much she admired him for more than his handsome features. She had better motives than that to fall in love with a person. She was deeper than that.

"We could fire Laino out the airlock once we start liftoff," Kor was saying. "That clears room for one more Annadian to pack on before we go."

She appreciated his attempt to make her smile, but his suggestion brought individuals to mind. The individual children who had been born on Annady whom Laino had wanted to exclude. The few aboard the Coronado were safe; she wouldn't let anyone come up with ploys and plots to get them out into the colony this evening.

"Why do you think the governor is so dead set against including any mixers or mixlings in the morning's lottery?" Khiry asked.

"I think he's a bigot."

The answer came simply and easily to Kor's lips. It acknowledged Khiry's fears. "Do you think they're all that way here?"

"What way?"

"Prejudiced. Do you think all the people we see moving among the buildings of this colony, scurrying about among the houses, gathering up their precious possessions…do you think they're all prejudiced like that? Do they all think of little babies made out of love between two species as something bad?"

Kor was quiet for a moment, as if thinking on the question. "I want to think they're not."

"Because you want to think the best of them?"

"Because some of them kept those babies among them. Crystal's daughter was protected enough in this colony that she and Mongoose could pick her up this morning. The governor was able to provide three mixlings for our doctors to study, and that means there are those children alive here. They haven't been murdered. They've been loved."

Khiry liked that explanation. It didn't make her decision easier, but it restored her faith in humanity.

Unfortunately, Kor kept talking.

"Of course, it's a little unsettling that the families were willing to hand three of those little kids over to our doctors for research. I mean, how do they know Devin and Dr. Max won't inject them with crap?"

"You're thinking of the Mengele Twins and horrible things from Earth's history," Khiry said. "Devin and Dr. Max are nothing like that."

"*We* know that. But these people don't. They willingly handed three very young children to our doctors, knowing our doctors wanted to study them because they're a mix of human and pangering. How messed up is this society?"

Khiry shook her head slightly. "I have to hope they recognized our doctors are good men. We're good people. We're here trying to find a way to help them get off this planet before a volcanic chain reaction of destruction…"

They paused a moment, watching a pair of colonists take turns swinging mallets against a short wall on the outskirts of the town; a wall too short to prevent lava from flowing into their streets and homes. The short wall called to mind the stones Kor had been helping the other colony build on a hill. Ultimately worthless against a tide of lava.

The urgency prevalent in the colonists' actions this evening bordered on psychotic. Where they had been experiencing worry before, they now experienced stark fear and terror. People randomly broke down in tears while they worked, while they packed, while they waited for Governor Laino and Cassidy Hopely to announce the lottery would be read at last.

"Or that governor gave them no choice," Kor suggested.

"I didn't want to think about that option."

"I don't trust him as far as I can throw him," Kor said.

"Neither do I. But we've got at least a handful of the children he would rather leave behind. We have Crystal and Delta on board with Jillian, Jessup, and Julia, which is most of a family that otherwise wouldn't be…" She let her voice trail as if that thought wasn't offering the comfort she wanted it to. "They're on the ship now. No matter what else happens, we've got some of these kids in a safe place. No one can force them off the ship without a fight."

She felt Kor's eyes watching her then, so she offered him a smile. "If the volcano should blow before we're ready, we've got at least a few people saved, right?"

He huffed. "That's one way to look at it, I guess. If that volcano blows again, and I mean really blows the way our sensors say it's going to, we'll be swarmed. I hope the five hundred names are already pulled, hope they're already on board, hope *we're* already on the ship, hope El already has it powered up, hope Maubry has the mix back in the engines…"

His voice faded away with her fading smile.

After they'd watched the shadows deepen for a while longer, she asked, "What if the morning comes?"

Kor frowned. "I don't think I understand."

She stared at the diminishing pink underlayer of clouds, watching the deeper tones of purple taking over in front of the chaotic star patterns representing the damning Debris Panel. "I wonder," she whispered. "I wonder what happens if the morning comes."

A chamber of her heart thudded a little harder at the thought that morning would never dawn for her again if she went through with the idea forming in her mind. She knew what she had to do. As captain, as leader, as the one who had taken the responsibility of command, she had to make the decision.

She closed her eyes and blew her breath gently out toward the stars above. Yes, it would be unfair to put this burden on anyone else. It would be selfish to ask anyone else to shoulder what she had been so proud of.

Her ship.

Her command.

Her decisions.

Her weapons mastery.

Her growth into whatever type of person she was becoming.

She hid the sadness and horror of it deep inside before opening her eyes and looking at Kor. "Yes. The morning. Let's get the crew back to quarters before it gets too chilly out here in this air. We'll get the cargo bay door closed to protect us from chill and crazy."

He accepted that reasoning without question, and they turned toward the ship.

"Captain," a woman called, approaching from the shadows outside the colony.

"Go ahead," Khiry told Kor. She waited for the woman and child who moved toward her in the shadows, thinking she recognized the colonist from earlier in the visit.

"Sally Cobbler?"

"Yes. Captain, I wonder if you would do some small favor for us?" Sally stopped and pulled what Khiry thought looked like Governor Laino's granddaughter to stand in front of her. She stood the child in front of her, facing Khiry with her hands on the girl's over-padded shoulders.

"What can I do for you?"

"Donna was born here, you know. She's never seen the inside of a spaceship. She'd like to spend the night with the kids in the infirmary, like a slumber party. Like the kids on Earth used to do when I was a little girl."

The request, coming from Sally, confused Khiry. The child appeared to be wearing a cloak, over a nightgown, over her clothes. Sally had dressed the girl in layers of clothes with an abundance of bracelets and hair pins; even her stuffed teddy bear wore a "belt" that was obviously a little girl's necklace.

"Isn't Donna the governor's granddaughter? Will he be upset if we let her spend a night playing with...you know..." Khiry couldn't bring herself to imply mixlings were any less than any other child. But she'd made a promise to change the meaning of the word. Thus, she straightened her back and said, "Will he be upset if she's allowed to play with other mixling children?"

"She's not his kin," Sally said. She placed a kiss on the calm, quiet child's head. "She's just his favorite little friend. And she just wants to have a slumber party with the other kids."

Khiry already shook her head to deny this request, but Sally forged ahead.

"I can't imagine Donna will get a warm welcome on Earth because of her lineage, Captain. Can you give her this one night of a real childhood memory?"

Khiry met Sally's eyes with supreme sadness. *This woman must know*, she thought. *She must somehow know what I'm going to do. She wants to save this child so badly that she'll give her up rather than see her starve under an ash cloud here on this horrible planet.*

With a small smile, Khiry held out a hand to Donna. "Of course. Lacy especially would be delighted to stay up telling stories…" She couldn't say another word for fear of choking on the lies they shared between them in the dusk.

Sally gulped back a sob. "Oh, praise God, thank you. Thank you."

Khiry put one finger to her lips to shush the woman. "Of course, of course. Say nothing of it."

*   *   *   *   *

Khiry had ordered the cargo bay door to be closed under the pretense of keeping the planet's chill out of the ship and any stray, multiplying spiders off the planet. Mutual benefit.

No one on the planet knew they'd gotten the pesky spider problem under control. And no one aboard the Coronado knew the captain sat in her quarters waiting for the quiet of the ship to signal everyone else slept.

No one heard her soft steps in engineering as she moved among the tubes, opening the mix doors so she could transfer components for electrolysis from her station on the bridge.

And no one heard her secure the locking mechanism on the bridge door. She sat alone with Onyx, the dragon who raised his head to watch her movements at the helmsman station.

While a certain solitude was necessary for this task, the weight of it made movement difficult. Walking to the pilot chair took monumental effort.

Waves of sorrow washed down her body, and her doe-brown eyes shone with tears threatening to blind her to the task at hand. With a teardrop splattering next to the docking clamp release, she gently, quietly, imperceptibly moved the lever forward and put the ship's startup sequence in motion.

Onyx watched with soulful dark eyes, offering a reassuring guttural whisper. Somehow, he understood the necessity of this. Somehow, he forgave her for leaving six thousand souls behind.

She offered the dragon a sad smile before powering the Coronado's engines into a soft purr. Captain Khiry Okerson was skilled. She'd run quiet operations for her family's ship when necessary. While the Coronado was larger than the ship her father had asked her to duck into and out of sticky situations, the concept remained the same.

Sneak away under the quiet of a cool, dark, threatening night.

Sneak toward a beautiful place of color named Misty Argoln's Dream.

And pray for calm when the morning comes.

The End

Watch for Khiry's next adventure in the Dragons in Space series:
Problems Between the Planets.
If you enjoyed this story, please share your opinion
at your favorite book-sharing site.

Appendix A

Vocabulary Helps

Language mutates over time in any society. While the adventure in *Problems in Annady's Core* takes place a mere sixty or so years in our future, changes in human life result in changes to language.

The speedy commercialization of space travel is one such change. The advances in space exploration that countries such as China, Russia, and Japan continued alongside the commercialization of space travel in the United States, the discovery of intelligent life beyond our galaxy, the increased rate of sea level rise (SLR) on Earth after 2030, and the usual addition of words with technology and societal change, means some of the characters in our story use terms a reader won't be familiar with. Here's a bit of vocabulary help.

Annady = *n.* (an a dee) a planet far beyond our solar system, made even more remote by its location beyond The Debris Panel

Bibliotecha = *n.* the electronic archive of articles, events, and stories shared via cyber-channels across the galaxies; the remains of Earth's Internet that the United Society for Peace and Strength (USPS) allows plus pangering documents that new race has granted us access to

Blender = *n.* a member of the resistance who stays on Earth and blends in

Debris Panel = *n.* a dangerous area of space that functions almost as a "net" wherein ships typically crash into fast-moving comets, stardust, and other obstructions

Dry = *adj.* not bad (if it's "dry," it's a good situation)

Earthling = *n.* an individual born on Earth and of the human race

Eldora Prime = *n.* a terraformed planet recently listed as uninhabitable (see Book 1); its moon is being terraformed successfully

EXSLR = *n.* exponential sea level rise (look up U.S. Geological Survey for a wealth of information about SLR predictions)

Graces = *n. pl.,* higher angels of the Panger System; you could think of them as similar to demi-gods from Greek mythology

Jump = *v.* leave a planet (usually refers to leaving Earth; a person "jumps Earth")

Jumper = *n.* a member of the resistance who leaves Earth to run errands, recruit other people to the resistance

Jute string = jute is a strong natural fiber made up of cellulose and lignin (mainly), which can be used to make coarse, burlap cloth; because jute is extremely common and affordable, to have string made of jute would be normal for the Coronado crew

Mercies = *n. pl.,* angels of the Panger System

Melon = *n., adj.,* idiot, stupid (a rude thing to call someone)

Mixer = *n.* an earthling who will date or even petition to marry an alien (non-earthling); at press time, no mixer marriages have been approved by the United Society for Peace and Strength (USPS)

Mixling = *n.* the product (or offspring) of a mixer relationship; what few mixlings have been born on Earth have had significant birth defects; most mixlings don't survive gestation and USPS science authority refuses to appoint a genetics committee to study the biology/science/fiduciary value of saving them

Pag = *v., n.* a naughty word, sexual in nature (*slightly* less offensive than peg)

Pangering = *n.* an individual born in the Panger System and of the Panger race

Path of annularity = the "track" (or shadowed portion of path) during an eclipse as one celestial body moves between the sun and the celestial body on which you're standing (check out the article "Ring of Fire Solar Eclipse 2020" by Joe Rao at space.com for cool information)

Peg = *v., n.* an obscene word for intimacy

Phoenix = *n.* a subspecies of dragon; about the size of a small horse on Earth, but with the scale coloration of a rock iguana

Resistance = *n.* a group of earthlings who wish to end terraforming on other planets; their reasons are myriad, but include a distrust of advanced alien races, and a desire to slow down the alliances with, and dependence upon, alien technology to solve Earth's overpopulation and SLR problems

Spang/spanged = *v.* shoot/kill with a gun of any kind

Tagger = *n.* a mercenary

That's dry = a phrase meaning "that's been lucky so far" or "that's brought good luck" (sometimes people say "that's not very dry," which means, "this is some bad luck right here")

Tighter = *n.* a prostitute

USPS = *n.* United Society for Peace and Strength (USPS) is a group of world governments on Earth that formed prior to the terraforming mandates of the early 21st Century; its Authority Customs Investigation (ACI) unit patrols the universe at this point, even commanding jurisdiction over Panger System ports

Wetting = *v.* getting bad (if it's "getting wetter," it's getting worse; this is a direct connection to the rising tides experienced after tectonic plates shifted, shores fell, and SLR sped up on Earth)

Wristplate = *n.* think of this device like a smartwatch with data storage capabilities; when you're in range of a planet's global positioning satellite (GPS) systems, or a ship or port station's bibliotecha, this timepiece-plus-communication device, worn on the wrist, allows you to pinpoint your location for mapping and search information; if you're not in range, you're out of luck; not all space travelers have wristplates because they tend to get broken when you're traveling around in space

Units of Measure

Astute readers will notice the crewmembers of the Coronado often think in terms of both International System of Units (SI) and Society of Automotive Engineers (SAE) units—also called English units.

You'll note that Electra, Khiry, and Kor hail from what used to be the United States, where the Imperial system from the United Kingdom remained popular into the 21st Century. Thus, crewmembers sometimes refer to distance in terms of feet or miles when on land.

Many other countries of Earth used the metric system (or SI) by the time our *Dragons in Space* stories take place. When earthlings worked out trade and cooperation with pangerings, the Panger System aliens easily adopted the SI system as the universal measurements to make communication, building, and parts-swapping efficient.

To help readers along, here are a few analogies and equations to keep in mind when reading.

32 degrees C is about 90 degrees F: For example, when Tempel Pliny goes into the Coronado's brig, the temperature of "more than 33 degrees C" is probably 95 and rising with humidity and no air movement. It's hot. It's uncomfortable. And that discomfort would hit him immediately.

There are 3 feet in a yard; 1 yard is almost 1 meter: When the Coronado parked 500 meters from the main colony of Annady, the ship was approximately 547 yards (or 5 and a half football fields) from the center, town hall structure.

1 kilometer is a little more than half a mile

Remember that a lightyear is a unit of distance, not time.

Appendix B

From the Master to his Alien Girl

By Governor Arbaseys Laino

No jury will acquit me
They cannot let me go
Evidence stacks against me
My obsession, they now know

  I am undone

No human will understand
Courts will convict without pause
No panger will take the stand
To speak for either of our cause

  I am undone

Euripides was right in the end
This dishonor I did not intend
My tendencies we cannot pretend
Could exonerate nor defend

  I am undone

Appendix C

Best Breathing Atmosphere Mix

At sea level, the atmosphere of Earth typically has the following compounds in the following amounts:

78.084% Nitrogen (N_2)

20.9476% Oxygen (O_2)

0.934% Argon (Ar)

0.0314% Carbon Dioxide (CO_2)

0.001818% Neon (Ne)

0.0002% Methane (CH_4)

0.000524% Helium (He)

The atmosphere can also contain up to 5% water vapor, and that's one of the big five gases (or compounds) usually present. In other words, at a single sampling of atmosphere around Earth, you'll at least find N_2, O_2, water vapor, Ar, and CO_2.

Those gases (or compounds) are the ones terraformers seek to replicate and keep at optimum levels in the atmosphere of planets or moons with comparable gravities to ours. In the novel *Problems in Annady's Core,* the geologists who selected the planet for colonization didn't dig deeply enough or study the rock long enough before sending humans to begin terraforming. (Readers familiar with the story in *Problems on Eldora Prime* will recognize that the same lack of research led to the horror there.)

A Scene from *Problems Between the Planets*

Book 4 in the Dragons in Space Series

Khiry slowly began to realize that light surrounded her. She hadn't opened her eyes yet, but the brightness seeped through her lids, as if warning her it would hurt.

Instead of blinding herself, she breathed in the antiseptic smell of peroxide and the harsh, wooden stink of betadine. She forced her eyes to remain closed and listened to metallic clanks of utensils hitting trays and paper-fabric shuffling against itself, as something draped in papery material moved nearby.

A man was speaking in English. "The only thing one of them that big will be good for is meat."

"Could sell them to a bio park," a woman suggested.

Their words confused Khiry. They didn't seem to fit with the new sound of a sphygmomanometer pumping, the hard squeeze tightening on her arm, and the smells of blood and iodine.

"I thought of that," the man grouched. It seemed to Khiry that he was offended by the woman's suggestion. "But there'll be too many questions to come along with a new species going to a government facility."

"New species? Who died and made you a zoologist all a'sudden?" the woman asked.

Something electronic near Khiry's head beeped quietly and the cuff on her arm began to hiss its slow release. *Automated,* she thought.

"Don't get cocky with me," the man said. "It's a real concern. You take a dragon into a government facility and people will want to know more about it than where'd you get it. They'll want background, history, habits, how to cage it, what to feed it, how to keep visiting school kids from getting roasted when they come to see it on display. You get my drift now? It's like taking a dinosaur in."

"A dinosaur?" she laughed. "When was the last time you transported a dinosaur?"

"When was the last time you transported a dragon?"

"Fine," the woman said. "I see what you're saying. But I think we'd get more from a bio park than a meat market. Meat market just pays by the pound."

Something clanked to a tray at the end of the woman's argument.

"Pays *more* by the pound for something rare that the elite want to sample," he argued back. "Your average bio park stooge wants something easy to put in a category and feed pre-packaged pellets. No muss, no fuss. You take a dragon in there and they'll pay less than they would for a pure-bred dog." He paused. "Per pound."

"All right. You made your point. You can drop the dragons off at a meat plant. I'm still working up these girls."

"I got a place in mind north of Vegas. But that tiny one might go into the pet market."

Khiry could feel the frown in the woman's voice when she asked, "like the smaller one?"

At this point, Khiry was ready to jump off the hard table she felt beneath her body and spang the two arguing over what to do with dragons. She'd figured out they had to be talking about her companions: Onyx, Nellie, Junior, Delta, and Goldie.

With more about the situation to assess, she kept her cool and waited to act. She could tell she lay under a sheet, but she couldn't feel any clothing; she'd rather not pop out naked in front of enemies and guards with no weapon.

Plus, the mention of "that tiny one" in reference to dragons piqued her interest. She'd only recently met Delta and Goldie on the doomed planet Annady, and even though they were smaller than Onyx and Nellie, she didn't think people would call them tiny. The idea of another species intrigued her, despite her situation, and made her wonder what else the two voices would bring up.

"Yeah," the man snorted. "It looks like it's a baby, but brokers are stupid enough to believe it if we tell them it's just another little dragon. What those Annadians coined a phoenix. They'll buy it and we'll be long gone before it starts growing big."

Khiry's heart stumbled over the mention of the people of Annady. How had this man talked to them? How did he know what they called the smaller dragons?

"And when it starts growing big?" the woman asked.

Khiry heard a rustle of fabric that she figured was the man shrugging his shoulders. "Not our problem," he said.

An intercom clicked and a computer voice said, "Captain Bane to the bridge."

The man she could now identify as Captain Bane muttered, as if to no one, "What the frack's wrong now?"

Khiry heard the hit of boots against the metal floor as he rose from whatever he'd been sitting on to her left.

"Hey, I assessed those two younger girls," the woman said. "No way they can carry yet. One of them is definitely mixed, part pangering, with birth defects inside that I can't figure out from just MRI."

"Fine. Pretty them up to sell in Vegas. Can you keep them pristine for three weeks?"

"Can do. But wait a minute. I've finished implanting the blonde, but do you see this girl? Do you know who she is?"

"Do I care?" the captain asked.

"She's Electra Endh."

"Whoa. Are you sure? Cassidy was right?"

"Of course, I'm sure. She's worth more than the rest of them combined. Do I implant her too?"

The air hummed with the electric buzz of lights and what Khiry now felt comfortable confirming as medical instruments. While she listened for Captain Bane's answer, Khiry did some quick deducing.

If Electra Endh was in the room with her, the blonde had to be Mongoose, but who were the two girls too young to conceive? Which of the children had been kidnapped? Where were the other members of the Coronado? What ship were they on now?

Las Vegas was on Earth and still famous for its decadence and immorality. If that's where they were headed, she needed to get her crew off this new ship; and it sounded like she had three weeks to do it.

"Yes," the captain said. "She's worth more if she's a proven breeder, no matter who she is."

Problems Between the Planets
by Fantasy Author Sandy Lender
will be available soon.
Follow Sandy Lender's author page
on Amazon.com for updates.

www.ingramcontent.com/pod-product-compliance
Lightning Source LLC
Chambersburg PA
CBHW070323130626
46556CB00007B/2711